Lady of Secrets

G.S. Carr

Brown Lady Publishing

Lady of Secrets

This a work of fiction. Names, characters, places, and incidents are products of the author's imagination or are used fictitiously and are not to be construed as real. Any resemblance to actual events, locales, organizations, or persons, living or dead, is entirely coincidental.

Brown Lady Publishing
PO Box 681385
Charlotte, NC 28216

Copyright © 2020 G.S. Carr
ISBN: 978-1-7344941-1-2
www.gscarr.com

To all the amazing women brave enough to stand out and claim their own adventure!

Chapter One

New York City, Summer 1861

Ten pairs of eyes exhibiting various levels of confusion and comprehension stared from sweat and grime-covered faces at the blackboard. German, Irish, and colored men and women sat side by side on the hard wooden schoolhouse benches, brought together by the common desire to improve their lives through education.

Some moved their lips, silently sounding out the passage scrawled in dusty chalk on the blackboard. Henrietta stood to the far-left side of it, allowing them an unobstructed view of the day's literature challenge. Since the start of classes two weeks ago, no one had correctly answered any challenge she'd given. Nevertheless, she enjoyed giving the students an opportunity to stretch themselves. The waning remnants of the sun's rays cast through the schoolhouse's glassless windows, inched down the blackboard marking the limited time the students had to give their final answers.

Henrietta stood at the front of the class, as she did every Tuesday and Thursday evening, her largest smile nearly splitting her face in two. She resisted the urge to fan herself, but it was no easy feat. Beads of sweat gathered in the fine hairs on her upper lip until they overflowed, dripping into her mouth. The salty moisture glided over her tongue, and although not the most appealing taste she'd encountered, at least it gave her something other than the sweltering heat to focus on.

Teaching classes during humid midsummer evenings were not the most ideal circumstances, but she gladly sacrificed her comfort for the sake of her students. After working ten to twelve-hour shifts at backbreaking jobs, most of them ambled into her classroom, weary yet eager to learn. If they could make it through a long day and sit in the stuffy schoolroom without losing their enthusiasm, then she could teach them with equal fervor.

Angling herself to remain out of the way of anyone still attempting to figure out the challenge, she read the phrase aloud. "Suffering has been stronger than all other teaching and has taught me to understand what your heart used to be. I have been bent and broken, but—I hope—into a better shape."

She paused, allowing her students the chance to digest what they'd heard. Every time she spoke those beautiful words, they sunk through her heart down into her soul. She hoped that one day her students would appreciate the full depth of the quote if they didn't already.

"Anyone? Can anyone tell me the author and title of the book that passage is from?" She scanned the room of silent individuals.

No one met her eyes. Each found a sudden fascination with their hands, their slates, the schoolhouse's barren wooden walls, or anything other than their teacher. She pursed her lips to suppress a laugh. Dusting the chalk from her hands, she smoothed them over the skirt of her dress, taking a moment to reign in her amusement before speaking. She waited until the need to laugh was under control, then opened her mouth to give a few encouraging words before repeating the question for the third

3

time. Before she could speak, a hand materialized in the air.

Her gaze trailed from the hand down to its owner's vivid sapphire-blue eyes. Flecks of honey sprinkled around the irises made them shimmer like twin oceans hiding golden treasure beneath their depths. This young man had reduced her to a mute statue when he'd set foot in her classroom for the first time last week. Having him now be the only soul brave enough to answer lifted her spirits for a different reason.

Not trusting her voice to be free of the heavy scratchiness of desire, she cleared her throat. Pushing her shoulders back and lifting her chin higher, she gestured in his direction. "Yes, Elijah. Do you know the answer?"

He lowered his hand, then nodded. "Charles Dickens, *Great Expectations*," he said, a hint of his Irish brogue coloring his Yankee accent.

The sound of his voice swept through her body, sizzling every nerve ending before mushrooming into a buzzing hive of warmth deep in her belly. If it weren't wildly inappropriate, she might have swooned, followed by combusting into a pool of liquid fire.

She relished his correct answer, and the excuse it gave her to unleash the full power of the exhilaration he invoked in her. "Correct, Elijah. Someone must have been paying close attention when I referred to my favorite author."

He replied with an unintelligible mumble before lowering his head and hunching closer to his desk to make notes in his grammar book. Wild strawberry color bloomed under the sandy cream skin of his ears and spread down his neck. Wisps of long, thick coral red escaped the confines of the ribbon holding his hair tied at the nape of his neck, slightly blocking his face.

Elijah squirmed in his chair. Henrietta gently bit the soft flesh of her bottom lip observing the nervous action. Swallowing down the trill in her voice, she cleared her throat for the second time. "Thank you for your participation."

No reply came. She watched the top of his head slowly rotate right, tracking the movement of his hand across the page as he wrote. Would it burn if she touched his mass of flaming waves? She snickered to herself at her rather banal musing. Attraction to a white man, even a poor immigrant, held a level of foolishness she should avoid. Attraction to a student held a level of moral compromise she couldn't cross. Placing her more carnal yearnings aside, she grabbed hold of her inappropriate thoughts and reengaged her "professional teacher persona."

Addressing the rest of the class, she said, "It would appear that Mr. Byrne is attempting to surpass you all with his participation. Even those of you who have been my students for much longer."

She gave a few students pointed stares, softened by gentle smiles. She could never be mad at the progress, or lack thereof, of any of her students. Their attendance at each lesson made pride well in her chest for every one of them. Although she was grateful for students like Elijah, who made it a point to contribute to class, each one of them held a hefty amount of her respect.

"All right, class. That will be all for this evening. There will be a spelling test during the next lesson. Please study your word list beforehand."

A chorus of thank yous and wishes for her to have a pleasant evening floated over the sound of books slamming shut and hurried feet shuffling toward the exit. She returned each greeting and waved at every student before they hastened out the door. The room emptied within seconds, except for the few students who usually stayed behind.

Mrs. Platt moseyed up to the board and squinted at the new vocabulary list. The poor woman's nose nearly wiped the chalk from the board, she stood so close. Mr. Johnson walked up to Henrietta, his wide grin displaying several empty spaces where teeth should have been. Deep crinkles in his leathery midnight skin fanned from the corners of his eyes, a testament to the unending joy he carried in his soul, despite the hardships life had dealt him.

Elijah marched up behind him, making himself the newest addition to her band of stragglers. Her eyes cut to him, lingering longer than they should, then darted back to Mr. Johnson. The older gentleman rocked on the balls and heels of his feet; his straw hat tilted to the side on his bald head. He tucked his hands in his overall pockets, all grins and good cheer. If he weren't nearly three times her age, she'd think he was sweet on her.

She rested her interlocked fingers on her stomach and pushed her shoulders back, straightening her spine. Using correct posture helped her adopt an air of authority yet openness.

"Hello, Mr. Jolly," she said, using the nickname she'd given him the first time he'd stayed after class to speak with her. "What joke do you have for me today?"

He pursed his lips, his eyes narrowing playfully. The ridge between his eyebrows rippled with enough waves to make even the most seasoned sailor seasick. "How you know I got a joke for you?"

He made an intimidating figure to those who didn't know him, standing over six-feet tall, with a sturdy, burly build for someone of his age. But Henrietta knew him, and she never missed the playful spark gleaming in his eyes.

"Considering you have a new joke for me after every class, the only logical conclusion I can draw when you walk up to me is that you have yet another to share."

"Shucks, you got a stunnin' beauty and a stunnin' mind. The boy that gets you as a wife will be a lucky fella indeed, Miss Retta."

Henrietta's joyful disposition faltered. The rigidness of her posture slackened, folding her shoulders forward ever so slightly. Her eyes flickered to the young man staring at his feet, pretending not to listen to their conversation, then back to Mr. Johnson. She laughed without humor, touching a hand to her face, but quickly lowered it. "Yes, well," she said, her voice flat. Her gaze darted around the room before settling on the collar of Mr. Johnson's faded white shirt.

"When that day arrives, I hope I am equally lucky in who I am saddled with."

Mr. Johnson's eyes softened. The merriment in them dimmed, making room for the seriousness of being empathetic to another's woes. Although the choice of her husband would be made to look like her own, in reality, it would not be. She was a free colored woman from a family of substantial financial means. Marriages in her social sphere were forged for legacy and alliances. Especially now, with the tensions among the states.

Henrietta pulled in a deep breath, using it to push her emotions into their proper place. Locked away behind a mask of contentment. She leaned toward Mr. Johnson, an eyebrow raised, and her practiced coy smile in place.

"But back to you, young man. Your flattery gets better each class. However, it won't win you any special favors."

Mr. Johnson's deep belly laugh, that only a man who truly loved being alive could produce, vibrated through the air. The contagious sound burrowed past the walls of her forlornness, genuinely lifting her spirits.

"I wouldn't dream of askin' for none. But couldn't pass up a chance to make a pretty lady happy."

"All right then. Let's hear your joke. I'm all ears."

That statement was partially true. Henrietta tried her best to listen to Mr. Johnson. But her eyes continued to wander over his shoulder to the scruffy Irishman waiting patiently for his turn to speak with her. His ill-fitting shirt, about a size too small, clung to the well-defined muscles of his arms, crafted from years of whatever laborious jobs he worked.

Part of her heart ached, knowing the fit of his shirt had more to do with lack of funds to procure a new one than a cocky desire to showcase his physical assets. The other part rejoiced at the unobstructed view of the appealing physique the fabric strained to cover. The build of most men in her social circles couldn't hold a candle to men such as Elijah. Many sported soft flabby middles from years spent living at the bottom of their cups and days filled with endeavors no more strenuous than arguing over the events covered in the morning paper.

Mr. Johnson's hearty laugh pulled her from her inappropriate gawking at the man she couldn't seem to look away from. Had he already told the joke? She joined in his cheery laughter, hoping the inflection in her voice didn't come across too forced.

"Well, I'll let you be. Thank you again for dat *superior* lesson," Mr. Johnson said.

Henrietta touched her fingers to her lips and dipped her head. Someone was eager to show they'd done the homework. It warmed her heart to watch the swell of pride her students had in themselves when they finally grasped a new concept she'd taught.

"Thank you for yet another wonderful laugh."

Mr. Johnson tipped the brim of his hat then followed the well-worn path his fellow students had already used to leave. She turned toward the blackboard to check on Mrs. Platt but found the space empty. She and Elijah were alone. No guardian. No chaperone. No one to keep her from stumbling over her words or behaving like a ninny in front of the man her mind couldn't convince her heart not to fancy.

Elijah stepped forward to occupy the space Mr. Johnson had vacated. A whiff of saltwater, sweat, and something spicy — ginger perhaps — wafted to her nostrils, quickening the pulse at the base of her neck.

He ran a hand over his hair to push the flyaway strands out of his face. "Excuse me, miss. Can... May I ask you a question?"

The teacher in Henrietta crowed over his correction. The woman in her wanted to turn tail and run like a skittish adolescent facing the first man she'd ever taken a liking to. What was wrong with her? She was a woman of twenty years, trained in the art of social graces, and drilled on how to carry herself with propriety no matter the circumstances. She could hold a conversation with a student without falling to pieces. Even one who made her forget her name every time his piercing jeweled eyes met hers.

She smoothed her hands down the front of her skirt and tried to take discreet, calming breaths. *Grab hold of yourself, woman.* She glanced up at him, fighting the breathy slow timbre that wanted to invade her voice. "Yes, of course, Elijah. How may I help you?"

"I have..." His voice trailed off, and his eyes squinted at Henrietta's face. "Pardon me, miss. You have something there." He rubbed next to his mouth with his thumb.

The stinging hot lashes of humiliation whipped up her neck and across her cheeks. *Perfection.* She stood before this exquisite specimen of a man with some sort of muck on her face. "Oh, dear." She quickly wiped the back of her hand over the spot he pointed out. "Is that better?"

The corners of Elijah's eyes crinkled. He flashed a dashing grin, revealing a cute dimple in his right cheek. "Made it worse. May I?"

He reached out but didn't touch her, waiting for permission. Seconds. Minutes. Hours. Henrietta wasn't sure of the amount of time it took to gather her wits enough to respond, but she was sure it was longer than necessary.

She nodded slowly. "Yes, thank you."

His warm, calloused hand gently cupped her face. Henrietta sucked in a sharp breath at the contact. The whisper of a sensuous shudder rippled through her. Perhaps he didn't mean it, but the soft stroke of his thumb over her skin felt more like a tender caress than an innocent, helpful gesture.

"There," he murmured, slowly grazing her cheek one last time. "It's gone."

"Thank you," Henrietta replied in a rasping voice. She blinked several times to break the spell he'd cast on her.

"You... You have a question, yes?"

"I do. I've been reading a new book." He pulled the hulking tome from behind his back and opened it to the page marked by several folds in the corner. "I don't understand this bit here."

He held the book out and angled it so Henrietta could read. She followed his finger to the paragraph in the middle of the page and read aloud. "'Have not many of us, in the weary way of life, felt, in some hours, how far easier it were to die than to live? The martyr, when faced even by a death of bodily anguish and horror, finds in the very terror of his doom a strong stimulant and tonic.'"

She stopped. Halted by both the black ashy line scrawled beneath the paragraph, as well as the brick wall her heart had slammed into, rendering it unable to beat and stealing her breath. She took a step closer and leaned in, her eyes blinking rapidly, unable to accept what they saw.

Chapter Two

"Is this...?" The question died in the haze of disbelief addling her mind. She gripped the book, turning it over to look at the front. Transfixed by the words printed in bold letters across the worn brown paper cover, her lips parted slightly. She lifted her head to stare into his eyes, searching them for the truth. "You're reading *Uncle Tom's Cabin*?"

He pulled the book back, then clutched it to his side in one hand, shoving the other into the pocket of his trousers. His eyes dropped to the floor. "I'm trying ta."

The lilt of his Irish ancestry took hold of his tongue, stripping away the practiced Yankee accent from his speech. He pulled at his collar, and his face flared red as the changing of a leaf in the fall.

This was the point in their interaction where she was supposed to resume her encouraging teacher smile and praise him for taking on the challenge of reading a book beyond the level of their lessons. She'd have to refrain from commenting on the contents of this particular title for the sake of staying away from divisive topics. But she couldn't pull her common sense past her curiosity. "Why? Why are you reading *this* book?"

His gaze flicked to hers, then back down to the ground. "I don't know. I... Never mind." He shrugged a shoulder, dismissing the rest of his thought and back-peddled away from her.

She reached out, capturing his arm in a gentle yet firm grip. She tilted her head so that her face was in his line of sight. Forcing him to look at her. "Please tell me," she said, her voice a soft plea.

"Thought it was important."

A pregnant silence conceived by the weight of his unspoken words settled between them. He opened his mouth, then closed it again, not breaking eye contact with her. He shifted his stance, his shoulders relaxing, and the tightness in his features ebbed away.

"They try to say we're different. Colored people and white people. But since I came to this country, they've been calling me names and trying to make me feel like I'm nothing. Rich men, men the same color as me, trying to force me into hard labor and pay me nothing for my work. We're all humans, no matter what they call us. I don't know what it's like to be a person with brown skin, but I figure I have more in common with a colored man than a rich one."

All sound faded away, drowned out by the deafening thud of her heart pummeling her ribcage trying to break free and leap into Elijah's hands. He understood. That she walked on two legs as did he. She had two eyes, one mouth, and two ears like him. And her heart beat, loved, and broke the same as his. He saw that she, and those who looked like her, were more than chattel.

Henrietta closed her eyes, reveling in the exhilaration of finding someone else who accepted the truth of her humanity. Moments like this were a balm on her ever-breaking heart. Reminding it to hold itself together a little while longer.

A solid warmth pressed against the front of her body. It seeped through her bones to the part of her soul that constantly fought the bitterness and icy emotional tundra of hate caused by the world. She wrapped her arms around the firm warmth and relaxed further into it.

Wait. One cannot touch a temperature, for it has no concrete form.

Henrietta's eyes popped open and collided with a worn cotton shirt pulled tight over the chest beneath it. The breath stalled in her lungs, and the scorching fires of hell the Reverend preached gleefully about every Sunday morning engulfed her.

Elijah held her, his arms encircled her waist, his chin resting against the top of her head. They stood so close it was a wonder he hadn't howled in pain from the burns he surely received touching her feverish skin. What were they doing? What was *she* doing?

"My dearest sunflower. Are you ready?" a honeyed baritone voice called from outside the schoolhouse doorway.

Henrietta leapt back, pulling away from Elijah so quickly that she caught the hem of her dress under the heel of her shoe and stumbled. Elijah caught her by the elbow, steadying her, but not before her hip struck the sharp corner of her desk. She winced and sucked in a hissing breath between clenched teeth.

"Are you..." he began, his brow wrinkling in concern..

But she held up a hand, cutting off the rest of his question, then stepped away "I'm fine, thank you."

Keeping a hand pressed against her injured hip, she straightened and took another, albeit smaller, step away. Good heavens. Too many more of these abrupt anxiety-inducing turns of events would send her to an early grave.

Matthew dashed through the front door, the tail of his coat flapping behind him. "What's going on? Are you all right?" he asked Henrietta.

"Yes, yes. I'm perfectly fine."

She tried for a reassuring countenance, which must have fallen short. He thrust the bouquet of daisies he'd brought into her hands then latched onto her shoulders. His deep brown eyes inspected from the top of Henrietta's head down to the hem of her skirt. She stood still, allowing him the time to examine her and put himself at ease. Although she didn't miss how his eyes lingered a bit too long on the round mounds beneath her blouse before moving along.

"I'm fine. I bumped my hip on my desk. That's all."

He concluded his examination with a decisive nod but didn't let go. His hands stroked up and down her arms, creating a jittery crawling sensation like a line of ants marching over her skin. How odd. Under normal circumstances, Matthew's touch neither excited nor repulsed her. But for the first time, she battled the impulse to shrug his hands off.

Her eyes darted to Elijah standing to the side, glaring at the ground. An uncomfortable warmth spread across her cheeks. What must he be thinking?

"Well, be careful next time. I can't have my precious sunflower getting all banged up," Matthew chided. His face relaxed, smoothing out the ripples in the brow of his unblemished toffee skin.

He placed a kiss on her forehead. This time, she couldn't resist taking a step back. Both hers and Matthew's eyes widened, staring at each other, equally shocked by her actions.

Matthew was her fate, and they both knew it.

He came from an upstanding free colored family who'd carved out a little piece of prosperity for themselves as tailors for some of the wealthiest white families in New York City. They'd owned a nice plot of land in Seneca Village until two years ago when the city purchased it for their large-scale public park project. Their mothers adored one another and visited regularly. Even if she didn't marry Matthew, it would be someone like him. At least she could tolerate his overall temperament and didn't find their conversations overly dull.

"I'll try my best," Henrietta said, recovering first. She fanned herself, needing to cool down from the sweltering heat that had nothing to do with the midsummer weather. "Thank you for coming to collect me. I'm almost finished answering a question from my student."

She gestured in Elijah's direction but kept her eyes averted. Meeting his gaze was not something the crushing embarrassment of the past several minutes would allow.

Matthew blinked several times then turned his head at a lumbering pace, like a disoriented bear waking from a long winter slumber and noticing a threat for the first time. Matthew frowned, his scrutinizing stare raking over Elijah from head to foot.

Elijah didn't fidget. He stood tall under the weight of the other man's assessment, his face a mask of indifference. As if whatever Matthew thought of him held as much significance as a fly buzzing around a pile of waste.

Matthew straightened to his full height. He lowered his chin, sneering down his nose at Elijah. Henrietta wanted to scoff at his trivial attempt to exhibit superiority. The modicum of his family's wealth, combined with the fine curly texture of his hair and smooth caramel toffee skin courtesy of an English great-grandfather, tended to heighten his sense of self-importance. Especially in the presence of runaway slaves and immigrants. It was the one thing about him Henrietta wished she could change.

"Yes, well," she said, taking a step to wedge herself between the two men. She addressed Elijah with her warm, albeit strained, smile. "We can continue..."

"Matthew Green," he said, cutting her off.

Elijah reached around Henrietta and stuck his hand out to Matthew. "Elijah Byrne."

Matthew glanced down at the offered hand. The corner of his mouth curled into an arrogant smirk. He kept his hands at his sides while his hard glare slowly slid back up to Elijah's face. He sniffed then wrinkled his nose as if an odor akin to death had suddenly assaulted it. "So, you're Irish? What do you do for work?"

Henrietta gasped. Her mouth hung open as she stared, eyes wide, at Matthew. How dare he try to embarrass one of her students like that? She placed her hands on her hips, her eyes narrowing into hard slits at him. "That's not..."

"Whatever I can to keep food in my stomach and clothes on my back," Elijah responded, cutting off her rebuke. "I'll load and unload a ship, shovel horse shite, fix a fence, or anything else that gives me an honest wage for an honest day's work."

The beginnings of a laugh tickled the back of Henrietta's throat. Elijah had thoroughly and eloquently put Matthew and all his high-handed haughtiness in his place. Part of her wanted to cheer and applaud him for doing so. She snuck a peek at Matthew, wanting to see his what a good humbling did to him. The vicious glint had vanished from his eyes, but to her disappointment, calculated appraisal replaced it, not shame.

"You may be the answer to a problem we were discussing earlier." Matthew eyed Elijah up and down as if assessing a prime buck that he might purchase. It wouldn't be surprising if he picked up one of Elijah's arms to better gauge his strength. "I'm sure you know the ins and outs of home repairs, general gardening and the like," he said with a flourishing wave of his hand in a circular motion.

Henrietta stared at Matthew as if he'd finally lost all traces of his sanity. What was he talking about? What had they been discussing earlier?

The shock, embarrassment, desire, mortification, and a myriad of other emotions she'd felt in the short span since the end of class clogged her brain, making it impossible to remember.

Elijah glanced at her, then back at Matthew. "I do."

Matthew winked at Henrietta, a self-satisfied smirk on his face as if he'd solved all the problems in her world. It came to her then. No! He couldn't. He wouldn't! Her mouth soured, then went dry.

"Excellent. Henrietta and her mother need to hire someone to help them with such things. Their last man decided he wanted to try his luck moving out west. They'll provide room and board in a guest house on the property. Would you be interested in such a position?"

The walls of her stomach squeezed violently, threatening to send its contents back up her throat. She held her hands up in protest. "Wait. He can't..."

"I'll take the job." Elijah cut her off.

Henrietta's eyes bounced between the two men as they carried on their conversation as if she were not standing there beside them. Men. It was her house. Her position to fill. Why did men think they had the right to take charge in a woman's life when she'd never asked for assistance?

She opened her mouth to tell them exactly that but closed it when a thought came to her. If Elijah took the job, he would live on her property. A stone's throw from her home. It was her duty to marry Matthew, so she would keep her distance from Elijah, but she wouldn't lie to herself and say it would be easy. Curiosity took hold of her tongue, rendering her incapable of protesting and ruining her chance of seeing what circumstances unfolded from having Elijah so near.

"Wonderful. And apologies for my earlier rudeness. I'm sure you can understand my leeriness of the man I find alone with my fiancé when I hear her in distress. I have to make sure my little sunflower is safe."

Henrietta winced at his use and overemphasis of the title fiancé. The summer heat must have melted the portion of her brain containing her common sense because she had to grit her teeth to keep the scathing correction that they were not betrothed from tumbling from her lips. He had neither asked nor received affirmation to the question of her being his wife, although they both knew that was the inevitable conclusion of their relationship.

Elijah dipped his chin in a curt nod to the other man. "Understood." He tucked the book he'd been holding in a white-knuckled grip under his arm, hiding the cover from view.

Perhaps she assigned more meaning to the gesture than she ought, but Henrietta felt as if Elijah had suddenly erected a wall between them. An unspoken pledge that from this day forth, she would be his employer and nothing more. Not that it was a bad thing. Henrietta had let her fantasies run wild for a moment, and now she could lock them away and return to her usual rational self. She crossed her arms over her middle, hugging herself to ward off the sudden chill that settled in her stomach.

Matthew pulled out his billfold and peeled off a dollar from the small wad of money, then handed it to Elijah. "Here. Take the ferry across the East River tomorrow morning at eight a.m. sharp. I will meet you at the docks to escort you to the home. If you do good work, the position will be yours."

"Thank you," Elijah said with a nod, accepting the offered bill.

He turned to Henrietta, a sultry undercurrent of liquid fire burning in his stormy midnight ocean eyes. As quickly as she'd seen it, Elijah closed it off behind a wall of cool restraint. A shiver went through Henrietta despite the stifling heat. Her gaze flickered to Matthew. If he noticed, he didn't show it. He had no idea what he'd done. Inviting a viper of temptation into the fragile folds of their courtship. The poor fool.

Elijah dipped his chin to Henrietta. "Thank you, Miss Wright, for your help. I'll see you again soon."

"You're welcome, Elijah," she said, her voice little more than a strained whisper.

He walked out the door before she finished her sentence.

Chapter Three

Two years later
New York, July 1863

Henrietta placed her hand in Elijah's, causing the usual spark of energy to sizzle up her arm, despite the glove keeping their skin from touching. Two years later and the flutter of desire still buzzed in her stomach whenever they were together.

"Thank you," she said as he handed her down from the carriage.

"Most welcome, ma'am." He reached back into the carriage and plucked a piece of pink silk, trimmed with black ribbon and lace, from the seat Henrietta had vacated. "Your bonnet."

Drat. Henrietta had promised herself she'd be better about not forgetting the blasted thing. Her mother insisted she wear it as a lady was never fully dressed without one. The itchy ribbon under her chin and the sweltering heat it trapped around her head were discomforts she simply had to endure for the sake of fashion and propriety.

"Thank you," she said, plucking the item from his outstretched hand.

As had become his custom since entering her employ instead of being her student, he kept his eyes averted when interacting with her. Henrietta sighed. Sometimes, she missed the ease of their previous relationship. Of being able to celebrate and show pleasure in his accomplishments. And the relaxed way he interacted with her.

She fiddled with her skirt to have something to do other than mourn what once was while she waited for him to help Abigail from the carriage.

"Yet again, Elijah, you've saved me from the impending fate of having my face meet the ground. The inevitable conclusion if I attempted to alight from the carriage myself." Abby dipped low in an awkward curtsy. Her head bent forward too much, nearly sending her tumbling over as if proving her need to be rescued from her own clumsiness. "My debt of gratitude gets larger every day."

Elijah's eyes twinkled with mirth. He returned the formal gesture with a bow. "It's my pleasure, Miss Abigail. Feels nice to be someone's savior every once in a while."

Henrietta bristled, her grip tightening on her reticule. "Come along now, Abby," she said in a curt tone. "We don't want to be rude and keep Mr. Bailey waiting."

It wasn't entirely true that Mr. Bailey awaited their arrival. He'd informed Henrietta at the time she placed her order that the book would be available for pickup any time that day. The true reason she hurried Abby along was to bring her and Elijah's cheery exchange to an end.

In truth, she wasn't mad at either of them. She was more upset with the circumstances that kept Elijah from calling her by her given name and engaging her in witty, or even not so witty, banter. Theirs was a relationship never meant to be. Even if he hadn't gone from being her student to her employee, his skin was too many shades lighter than her own. Why did life have to be so complicated?

She scampered into the brick bookshop, ready to be away from the irrational emotions laying siege to her mood. Abby quickly caught up with her and walked silently by her side. The slight skip in her step warned Henrietta that the quiet wouldn't last long.

"Soooo..." Abby said, proving Henrietta's assumption correct. "Want to talk about your rather sour disposition back there?"

Henrietta's nose rose higher in the air, her posture becoming more rigid. "I haven't the slightest clue what you mean."

"Oh?" Abby's tinkling giggle rang between them. "You don't recall your fit of jealousy that happened only seconds ago?"

"It wasn't jealousy. It was..." Henrietta couldn't finish the sentence. Jealousy was exactly what she'd been feeling. "It wasn't for the reason you think. Sometimes I... I wish things could be different."

"I know what you mean."

Henrietta met Abby's gaze, which was brimming with understanding. Of all people, she knew her friend truly grasped the burden of having one's desires, and one's reality be in complete opposition. Abby had only ever had eyes for Russell Bell. Unfortunately, the pathetic lout couldn't pull his head from his nether region long enough to see the sparkling diamond beneath Abby's homely exterior.

The poor girl lamented about her unrequited love *ad nauseam*. Henrietta prayed for the day when a man would look past Abby's thick spectacles, ghostly pale skin, and frizzy brown hair that she refused to tame because, in her words, "What's the use? Nothing can be done to make my hair appealing. The color is so dull it resembles a mud puddle." Whoever that man was, he'd be blessed with an intelligent, funny, and caring woman by his side.

They walked through the store to the counter in silence. Both women were too steeped in their myriad of anguish to muster the motivation needed to drum up a conversation. A young man stood behind the register, hunched over with his elbows resting on the wooden counter. His attention was riveted on a copy of *The Revolt*. Henrietta wrinkled her nose at the anti-abolitionist paper that spouted lies and propaganda about the many ills freed slaves would wreak on the Northern economy and labor market.

The young man's dusty blond head stayed bent even after Henrietta and Abby stopped in front of the counter. Seconds ticked by, leaving the two ladies waiting for the greeting he'd yet to give. Henrietta had never seen him before, which meant he must have started working at the bookstore within the past week or so. Perhaps Mr. Bailey had forgotten to train him on the proper etiquette of dealing with customers.

Abby cleared her throat, drawing the clerk's attention to them. His eyes flicked from her to Henrietta, annoyance emanating from his cool gaze.

"Yes?" he finally said.

One word. One curt, rude word. That was how this ragamuffin saw fit to greet a customer who'd come to spend money in this shop.

Henrietta let his impolite address go. "I've come to collect the book Mr. Bailey procured for me. He said it would be ready today."

"You can read?" The clerk asked in a voice laced with mocking venom. His brows drawn close together and his tightened expression aired his skepticism of her ability to do so.

Henrietta and Abby gasped in unison, both so shocked by his blatant disrespect that their mouths fell open in disbelief. Never in all her years of patronage to this bookshop had anyone spoken to Henrietta in such a manner. She almost didn't know what to do.

"How dare you say such a thing to her?" Abby seethed, recovering first. Her pale skin finally gained some color, taking on a splotchy crimson hue.

The young man straightened and crossed his arms over his chest. Ignoring Abby's outburst, his piercing gaze bore into Henrietta, tearing through her pride. "Well, can you? Here, read this." He flipped the paper around and shoved it across the counter at her.

"Wha... Of... Yes, I can read!" she sputtered, anger and humiliation, stealing her composure. "Hence, my presence in this shop to retrieve my book. If..."

"Good men are dying every day for you people when they should be at home safe, taking care of their families. Being forced to fight for something they don't believe in. For what? So that Negros can come up here and take jobs from hardworking white men and drive down our wages?"

Ah, so this was the root of his issue. Anger over a war Henrietta had no hand in starting, although she was glad it had begun. Perhaps he even had a brother or cousin who'd fought and lost their life.

Abby took a menacing step forward, her hands balled into fists at her side. Henrietta held out her arm, blocking her advance on the scrawny young man. No doubt Abby was ready to swing a right hook at the side of his head in defense of Henrietta's honor. But Henrietta wouldn't let her friend do that. He was only a wounded person lashing out.

"I've come into this shop to retrieve my book," Henrietta said, her voice calm. "If you do not feel inclined to offer me assistance, then please get Mr. Bailey so he can do so."

"He's busy," the boy hissed. His nostrils flared with the force of his heavy breaths. Then, as if someone had flipped a switch on his personality, his demeanor calmed, filling with pleasant hospitality. "Ah, good day, sir. How may I help you today?"

Henrietta and Abby whipped around to see who he had spoken to. Elijah strolled through the front door, a polite smile trained on the shopkeeper. So, that was how the clerk wanted to play this. He'd probably never help Henrietta, no matter how polite she was to him.

"Oh, I've only come to..."

"Elijah, we are leaving at once," Henrietta interrupted him, pivoting on her heels then marching to the door.

She'd had enough insult heaped upon her today to last several lifetimes. As much as she wanted to devour her latest literary acquisition, she could wait until Mr. Bailey was there to help her.

"Don't you dare speak to him like that," the clerk snapped. "Show some respect when speaking to your betters."

Henrietta whirled around, ready to give this corny-faced fool a piece of her mind. "I will..."

Elijah wrapped his large hand around her rigid finger pointed at the clerk, and lowered it to her side. He stepped in front of her, anger rolling off his taut muscles. "She can speak to me anyway she damn well pleases. And considering I work for her family, I'd say she is my better, not the other way 'round. Now apologize before I rip your pompous head off and shove it up your narrow arse."

All the outrage drained from Henrietta, leaving her a weak-kneed jumbled mess of quickened breaths and sensitive skin that wanted to touch and be touched by Elijah. He'd threatened a man for her. Call her daft, but the protective gesture had her fighting a smile that could rival the brilliance of the sun. She pressed her hands to her belly, afraid the giddy emotions fluttering inside her would carry her away.

Abby nudged Henrietta with her elbow. As much as she didn't want to peel her eyes away from Elijah, Henrietta gave her friend her full attention. Barely. Abby waggled her eyebrows suggestively and fanned herself in a dramatic show of encouragement.

"I... Um..." the young man sputtered, bring the harshness of reality crashing back down around them.

"What's all that ruckus about?" Mr. Bailey hobbled from the back of the bookshop, the limp in his left leg more pronounced as he tried to move at a quickened pace.

The clerk pointed an accusatory finger at Henrietta. "This Nig..."

"Don't you dare finish that sentence," Elijah seethed, pressing into the young man's space until he shrunk back, his round eyes brimming with terror.

"You watch your tongue, George," Mr. Bailey barked, his own eyes going wide with shock over what the clerk was about to say. "Do you know who this woman is?"

"But I..."

"No buts. Why don't you go make yourself useful and count the inventory? Start at the back of the store and work your way up."

Mr. Bailey's heated glare followed George until he was a good distance down a row of bookshelves. Then he took Henrietta's smooth hands in his pale wrinkly ones, his expression softening. "I apologize for George's behavior. I'm not sure what he said, but I assure you I'll deal with him later."

It wasn't hard for Henrietta to regain her jovial disposition for the kind older man. Her heart still soared from the way Elijah had scolded George on her behalf. Not that she'd doubted he would, but a chance had never presented itself for him to do so.

Men who were sweet on a woman did such actions.

"No problem at all, Mr. Bailey," she said, her voice a little too bright. "Although I thank you for your apology."

"Anything for my best customer." He patted her hands before letting them go and limping behind the counter. "I have your book right here. *The Count of Monte Cristo* by Alexander Dumas."

"Thank you so much." Henrietta cradled the book lovingly against her chest. She'd devoured *The Three Musketeers* in a matter of days and couldn't wait to start on his one.

"I hope you enjoy it. I've heard great things. Full of drama and adventure."

"I'm sure I will. Thank you."

"Any time. Let me know if I can get anything else for you."

"I will. Good day, Mr. Bailey."

"Good day, Miss Wright."

Henrietta and Abby waved, then turned to leave. Elijah followed close on their heels. There were so many things she wanted to say to him. Offer her gratitude, for one. Maybe confess that what he'd done made her want to throw her arms around his neck and hug him close.

Instead, she turned to Abby and said, "We should hurry. We still have three more shops to visit before heading home."

"Lead the way."

Emotions forced behind a mask of propriety, she did exactly that. Steered them away from everything she wanted to say but didn't have the courage to speak aloud.

Chapter Four

Elijah lay in the freshly cut grass, his arms tucked beneath his head, and stared up at the stars glittering overhead. They illuminated the midnight sky and lit the way through the darkness for the men and women below. For some, their light represented a compass by which to navigate toward freedom. For others, their light guided the path to an awaiting lover, ready to steal late-night kisses.

To Elijah, they were a representation of how small he was in the grand design of the universe. No matter how difficult his life became, he looked to the sky and found reassurance that there must be a bigger purpose to his life.

Everything he experienced had meaning, even if he couldn't see it.

The soft pad of light footsteps across the grass broke through his moment of introspection. He sat up, the tempo of his heartbeat quickening the way it always did when she was near.

"I hope I'm not intruding," Henrietta said as she strolled up beside him.

You could never intrude because every second I get to share with you is one I cherish. I look forward to being in your presence as much as my next breath.

"Not at all."

He watched her gracefully lower herself to the ground, then tuck her legs beneath her bottom. She'd fixed her hair in a single plait that hung down the middle of her back. Moonlight reflected off her rich copper skin, giving it a delicate glow. The frills of her high-necked nightgown protruded from the collar of her powder-blue wrapper, cinched tight around her slim waist by an elaborately embroidered cloth belt. She put him in mind of a fairy from the Irish folklore his father used to tell him about. Heaven help him—he wanted to run the pads of his fingers against her smooth skin until he memorized its silky texture.

"Can't sleep?" he asked when she finally settled.

He probably should have asked her a different question. Like why she was sitting next to him at such a late hour. And why she did so dressed in her nightclothes. But he didn't care about anything other than having her near.

A sheepish grin transformed her beautiful face into a masterpiece of alluring femininity. "I admit the intriguing world Alexander Dumas crafted in my newest literary confection has kept me captivated for several hours now. The need to change my reading candle was the only reason I stopped. When I peeked out my window and saw you here in the garden, I decided to do something I should have done earlier."

Elijah bent his knee to rest his elbow on it, then propped his head on his knuckles, giving her his full attention. "And what might that be?"

"Say thank you." She reached out and touched his arm. "Thank you for the way you stood up for me today to that horrid clerk."

Her gaze was sincere and unwavering as she spoke. That alone stole the breath from Elijah's lungs. The feel of her warm, soft hand on his arm sapped the moisture from his mouth, making his tongue momentarily useless.

"No," he said when he remembered how to speak.

"No?" Henrietta repeated, tilting her head and glancing around them as if searching for a hidden meaning in the single word.

He covered her hand with his own. "Never thank me for doing what I should as a man who..." His runaway emotions almost made him reveal truths he wasn't ready to share. "You never have to thank me for treating you with respect and making sure others do the same."

"Thank you for saying that. You're a good man, Elijah."

"I'm only doing what's right. Nothing special."

"Choosing to do what's right when most people don't is a very special quality for a man to have. Especially in the eyes of those who benefit from those choices."

The only reply Elijah could give was an accepting grunt. It burned him up that her statement held so much truth. Men and women turned their backs on doing the right thing every day in this country, which was why it was being torn apart by war. Such was the plight of men. Greed and the desire for power had tainted men's hearts throughout history.

Silence descended upon them. Henrietta pulled her hand from his and dropped her gaze to the ground. She moved her braid from one shoulder to the other, then smoothed a hand over it. Elijah watched her, at a loss for words. He should say something. Anything to keep her talking and seated next to him. Soon the silence would move from idle to awkward and unsettling. Then she would rise and leave him.

"I..."

"Do you..."

They both spoke, jumbling their words together. They clamped their mouths shut, each averting their eyes. A warm flush crept up Elijah's neck and over his ears at the blunder.

"I'm sorry," he said, speaking again first. "What were you going to say?"

"Oh, nothing. I..." Henrietta let her sentence trail off, leaving him in torturous suspense. She nibbled her bottom lip and wrapped her arms around herself as if warding off a chill. Letting her arms fall to her sides, she plastered on a weak smile and finally said, "I wanted to see if you could take me to Ruth's house tomorrow. Well, later today, I suppose. It's our weekly card game."

"Yes, I can," Elijah said, his voice tinged with disappointment.

"Thank you."

There was something else she wanted to tell him. He could sense the unspoken message locked inside her heart as if it called out to him. Even after he agreed to her request, she didn't move. She stared at him, watching and waiting. But for what? What did she want to hear? He wished he knew so he could deliver the words.

Could she possibly be waiting for him to announce the truth of his feelings for her? No. She'd never wish to hear such things from him. She was a priceless treasure well outside the reach of his calloused, dirt-stained hands. She came from money, was well educated, and her family was well connected. She was everything he wasn't. And everything he'd be stupid to think he could have.

"Good night, Henrietta."

Her expression fell. Did he dare hope that she was disappointed that their conversation had ended?

"Good night, Elijah."

With the lithe grace of a woman trained in the art of poise and elegance, Henrietta rose from beside him. A cold emptiness enveloped Elijah as soon as she took the first step away. He wanted to call her back to him and say... What exactly did he want to say? What could he say?

That she'd consumed his thoughts and dreams every day and night for the past two years. That he wished he was worthy of her. That he treasured each of her smiles and stored them in a special chamber of his heart that he visited whenever he needed to feel something good.

Her small feet traipsed noiselessly across the grass, but each step she took away from him was like the echoing boom of a closing window of opportunity. He watched her until she entered her house. Before closing the door, she turned back and waved at him. He stored the image of her standing in the doorway, cloaked in moonlight, in his memory. She was the woman he would always want but could never have.

"Don't be stingy. Pass the bottle already," Ruth demanded, her voice slurred by the large amounts of whiskey she'd already consumed, and the fat cigar wedged between her teeth.

"Hold on, you glutenous cow," Abby snapped back. "I've barely poured half a sip in my glass."

Henrietta snickered at her friends' drunken squabble. Neither could hold their cups, which always made for an entertaining time during their weekly card games. She didn't have much room to criticize, though. She was already halfway to being good and corned herself.

Abby passed Ruth the bottle of Old Crow bourbon whiskey, with a sloppy scowl on her blotchy pink face. Ruth plucked the cigar from her mouth and blew a dense puff of smoke before setting it on the tray beside her elbow. She swiped the whiskey from Abby's hand and brought the bottle to her mouth, tossing the amber liquid down her throat.

"Eww. You disgusting heathen," Abby grossed. "We still want some of that. Why d'you go and put your nasty lips on it?"

"Because I wanted to, and I can. Now hush up and deal."

Abby picked up the deck of cards and dealt, grumbling the entire time under her breath about Ruth's lack of manners.

"No, not to me first. Deal to the left. To Retta."

"Don't tell me what to do. I know what I'm doing."

Abby snatched up the cards she'd already laid down and shoved them to the bottom of the deck. Adding a monologue about ungratefulness to her rant, she re-dealt the cards in the direction Ruth had pointed out.

"Look at you now," Ruth complained again. "We're playing *Three* Card Brag. The number of cards to hand out is in the name. Three, not four. Give me those."

Ruth grabbed hold of the deck, but Abby refused to let go. They tugged the cards back and forth, heckling and calling each other all manner of foul creatures and uncouth barbarians. Henrietta drummed her fingers on the table, waiting for them to finish their squabble. Eventually, Ruth wrestled the deck from Abby's iron-fisted grip, then stuck her tongue out in smug victory.

Abby wagged a stiff finger in Ruth's face. "Oh, you... you..."

"Me, me, what? Your mind's so addled you can't even come up with a good insult. Further proof I should do it."

"So, ladies, what are your thoughts on the lottery this Saturday?" The back and forth had become too much for Henrietta. If her friends didn't take the bait and change the subject, she might call the evening to a close. Which would be a pity, since she'd won the last two games they'd played. Ruth and Abby were horrible gamblers when they were sober, and adding alcohol to the mix increased Henrietta's odds of winning by nearly half.

"Lottery?" Ruth asked.

Now it was Abby's turn to don an air of superiority. "She means the lottery to draft soldiers. You know, the new requirement under the new conscription law. Really, Ruth, do keep up with the state of your nation."

"I keep up with..."

"I think," Abby shouted over Ruth, "it's an even bigger tragedy than Ruth's vile lips on the *shared* liquor bottle. The government is whining about their need for men to fight, yet they allow a clause for wealthy men to buy their way out of service. It's all a bunch of highfalutin crockery if you ask me."

"Couldn't agree more," Ruth stated with a resolute nod. "If you ask me, they ought to let women join the army. We're better strategists, we can multitask, and we're much better liars. We could end the war in weeks if not days."

"Exactly!" Abby chimed in. "Countless women look their balding, potbelly husbands in the face every day and tell him he's the most virile, strapping example of a man they've ever seen."

All three women dissolved into fits of unrestrained hysterical laughter. Henrietta could imagine the whipping men's egos would take if women did, in fact, join the military and outshined them. Women balanced the duties of being wives, mothers, and stewards of their households every day. They very well could do a better job of ending the war than men.

"We should join," Henrietta said between bouts of laughter. "Even if all women can't join, three can still give the Union a much better chance of winning."

Ruth's face lit up, her expression akin to an exaggerated political cartoon. She nodded enthusiastically at Henrietta's suggestion. "Yes! We should. Retta is right. We could help. We don't have to be soldiers, but we can do something." She picked up the bottle of whiskey and poured a hearty shot in each of their cups. The amber liquid sloshed over the rim of her glass when she stood and hoisted it in the air, out over the table. "Let's do it! Who's with me?"

Abby was the first to rise and hold out her cup next to Ruth's. "I help my brother attend to his patients all the time. Maybe I can be a medic on the battlefield."

Henrietta's skeptical gaze bounced between her friends. Each wore nearly identical expressions of zealous, borderline demented, enthusiasm at being active participants in the war among the states. Clearly, they'd had more to drink than they should've if they were making such silly declarations. But she'd started it, and neither of them would remember this in the morning.

She raised her glass, thrusting it between Ruth and Abby's wobbling cups. "All right then. Let's join the military!"

"Whoo!" Ruth crowed. "Blue always looked good on me, anyway."

Ruth flung her thick black braids over her shoulder, then swished the skirt of her dress back and forth like she was a Parisian socialite wearing the season's latest fashions. Henrietta and Abby's shoulders shook with the force of their laughter at their vivacious comrade's antics.

"That makes one of us. Gives my skin a more ghostly pallor than usual," Abby said, waving a hand in front of her pale face. "Now let's get this over with. My arm is tired."

They nearly missed but made their glasses collide over the middle of the table, sealing their bargain with a drunken toast. Henrietta laughed with them, grateful for moments like these. They were so different yet loved each other like actual sisters. Tonight would definitely go down as one of the most entertaining evenings of their lives. Too bad Ruth and Abby wouldn't remember it.

Henrietta picked up the forgotten cards Ruth had dealt. "Back to the evening's original agenda. Who's ready to lose all their money?"

Chapter Five

Elijah lifted his nose in the air and inhaled a long glorious whiff of roasted chicken and cornbread. His mouth flooded like a slobbering dog anticipating its next meal. The delicious aroma wafted through the open kitchen door, filing the wide hallway and setting his stomach off in an angry grumble.

He slowed his steps as he neared the kitchen doorway. What was Mrs. Lewis preparing tonight? The woman was arguably the best cook in the state of New York. Maybe in all the northern states. Even on her worst cooking day, no one could make a dish that held a candle to her secret family recipe chili. Everything she'd made to date had left his toes curled in satisfaction.

Elijah peeked through the doorway then halted at the sight before him. Instead of Mrs. Lewis dipping a wooden spoon into a giant cast-iron pot, hand on her ample hip while humming to herself, he saw another equally amusing spectacle.

Ruth, Abby, and Henrietta were huddled together, their expressions epitomizing angry storm clouds. Fingers pointed at each other, they strained to keep quiet while talking over one another.

"We were drunk! I didn't mean it," Henrietta hissed between clenched teeth.

"Yes, we were, but we meant every word," Ruth replied, pointing between herself and Abby, who stood next to her nodding in agreement.

"You can't possibly think..."

"We can, and we do," Abby cut in. "It's the only reason we're here tonight. Your uncle is part of the Black Militia for Union Victory. Talk to him. He can help us."

"No!"

"Yes!" Ruth and Abby shouted in unison.

As entertaining as it was to watch this rather lively falling out, Elijah took his cue to step in.

He could sense the potential explosion of their friendship. Whatever was happening between them now, under normal circumstances, neither of them would want to happen.

"What are you ladies up to?" he asked, entering the kitchen.

"Nothing," all three women said at the same time.

Elijah stuck his hands in his pockets and looked at each woman in turn. "Didn't sound like nothing. Sounded like a whole bunch of something."

"Yes, well," Henrietta rushed out. She folded her hands in front of her, then released them, then folded them behind her back. "Ruth and Abby were—"

"Telling Retta how much we're looking forward to speaking with her Uncle Paul," Ruth cut in. "It's been so long since we last spoke to him."

"So very long," Abby agreed with an overly bright smile. "Which is why we should get going. Everyone is probably waiting for us to join them so we can begin the meal. Let's not dally any longer."

Abby marched off, and Ruth followed closely behind. They each gave Elijah sugary sweet smiles that on anyone else would have appeared innocent. On those two, it put him in mind of deviant miscreants up to no good. Elijah bit the inside of his mouth to keep from laughing outright.

Henrietta closed her eyes and pinched the bridge of her nose. "Remind me why I continue to associate with them."

"Because you love them as much as they love you. And no matter how vexing they are, you can't imagine life without them."

She exhaled a drawn-out, exasperated breath. When her eyes opened again, she forced an overabundance of cheerfulness into her tight expression. "Right. Well then, I guess we should get to dinner. And thank you for stepping into our little disagreement."

"Any time. Shall we?" Elijah extended his elbow for Henrietta to take. It was a gamble. They hadn't shared such a friendly interaction since he'd come under her family's employ, but their conversation last night gave him hope. It was the most they'd spoken in the past two years. They would never be lovers or share anything deeply intimate, but perhaps they could become friends.

Henrietta's gaze dropped to his offered arm, then rose to meet his. "Yes, thank you."

Elijah nearly crowed out loud when she wrapped her gentle hands around his arm. Yes, maybe one day, they could find their way to an amicable friendship. If his stubborn heart didn't ruin it by wanting something more.

Forks and knives scraped across dinner plates as everyone devoured their meal in silence. Henrietta wasn't sure what new ingredient Mrs. Lewis had used to cook the chicken, but the meat was so succulent and flavorful that the minutes of quiet eating had stretched on longer than usual. By now, she or her mother should have started an easygoing line of conversation, but neither could take their fork out of their mouths long enough to do so.

Plate finally empty, Henrietta lifted the napkin from her lap and wiped her lips. "I must say, that was the best meal I've had in a very long time."

"I couldn't agree more," her mother chimed in from the head of the table. "I'll have to tell Mrs. Lewis to add it to the menu more often."

"Quite delicious," Thomas added in. "It's unfortunate the brave men fighting on the front lines don't have the luxury of such meals while men like me sit around not helping them claim freedom for all people."

Henrietta shook her head at her cousin's dramatic soliloquy. At seventeen, he swore he was a man who needed to partake in the glory of battle. If one didn't know any better, it would be easy to assume he had a death wish.

"That means we should be even more grateful for this meal," Uncle Paul responded in a cool tone, not looking at his son.

"Or it means you need to let me be a man and fight next to my brothers."

"Last I checked, I only had one son," Uncle Paul quipped, earning a round of snickers from everyone around the table. "My answer hasn't changed from the previous time you brought up the subject. No. The front lines are no place for you."

Thomas threw down his utensils and leaned on his elbow across the table. "But I'm..."

Uncle Paul slammed his palm against the table. "End of discussion. Do not ruin your aunt's lovely dinner with your incessant moaning about fighting. It won't happen."

"You can't keep me sheltered forever. A man fights to protect his home. He fights to defend those who cannot defend themselves. You taught me that."

"No, Thomas! I will not watch you throw away your life on some filthy, blood-soaked battlefield. War is not some young man's fantasy quest for glory and honor. It's a hard, disgusting, soul-stealing undertaking. The chance of disease taking you is just as high, if not higher, than a bullet."

"You act as if my death is guaranteed. Has it ever occurred to you that I might survive?"

"Survival in battle is guaranteed to no man. The only place your life is guaranteed is in the safety of our home. Besides, even if your body endures, your mind may not."

"Enough, gentleman," Henrietta's mother cut in, voice filled with the infallible poise and authority of a queen. "Thomas, your father is trying to protect you, as is his duty as your sole caregiver. Your foolish youthful pride is clouding your ability to see the love beneath his actions, but that doesn't mean it isn't there. Now, if you will please refrain from mentioning more about fighting and the war while in my home, I would appreciate it."

Thomas folded his arms on the table, his posture slumped and defeated. "Pardon my rudeness, ma'am." He picked up his fork and pushed chunks of potato around on his plate.

"All is forgiven. And Henrietta, do sit up, dear. Elbows off the table."

"Yes, ma'am."

Henrietta quickly complied with her mother's mandates. It was always best to do as you were told when she got in one of these moods. Thomas had brought discord into Martha Wright's home. A grievance she wouldn't tolerate; civilized members of society never engaged in such base behaviors.

"Well, that was such a lovely meal," Ruth said, ignoring the stifling tension engulfing the room. "I'm rather stuffed. Should we move to the sitting room for drinks and light conversation?" Her pointed gaze locked on Henrietta, then traveled slowly to Uncle Paul.

Henrietta yawned behind her hand. "I have to admit to being rather tired. If you all would excuse me, I need to retire early for the evening."

She remained seated, awaiting her mother's permission to be excused. Leaving in the middle of a dinner party with so many guests was rather rude, and something Henrietta normally wouldn't do. Her mother's shrewd gaze swept over her, no doubt searching for signs of anything other than fatigue being the culprit of her abrupt departure. Henrietta breathed a sigh of relief when her mother gave her a barely perceptible nod.

"Sleep well, my dear."

Ruth and Abby sent Henrietta murderous glares. Was she running away from their harebrained promise? Yes! What person with half a mind wouldn't? War was dangerous. Why would a person who didn't have to participate volunteer to join in the carnage? Henrietta pushed back her chair, ready to make her escape.

"Oh, wait!" Ruth said as if something important had suddenly popped into her head. "Henrietta, you wanted me to remind you that you had something important you needed to speak with your uncle about. Good thing I remembered before you took your leave."

Five pairs of eyes fell on Henrietta. Three with genuine curiosity. One with suspicion. And one with conspiratorial glee.

Uncle Paul swallowed his last bite of food, then wiped his mouth. "What do you wish to speak with me about, my dear?"

"I was hoping we could have a private conversation."

"Since we're all finished," her mother chimed in, "how about the rest of us retire to the parlor for coffee and tea, while you two walk around the garden?"

"Splendid idea, Mother. We shouldn't be gone long."

Chairs scraped across the hardwood floor as everyone stood to move on to their next destination. Henrietta took small steps, her hands folded in front of her, fingers fidgeting to channel the nervous energy from having to ask her uncle to let her join his efforts to aid the Union army. She could feel the weight of Elijah's curiosity on her, despite not looking in his direction. He might not know exactly what she and her friends were up to, but he no doubt had his suspicions it wasn't anything good.

The previously delicious meal soured and churned in her stomach. She rubbed the fabric of her skirt between her fingers until a new thought came to her. Chances were high that Uncle Paul would tell her no. He'd denied Thomas's repeated pleas to join the military, and he would more than likely deny her request to join the Black Militia for Union Victory. He wouldn't want her in danger. With a reassuring lightness in her step, she strolled to the garden, ready to hear the denial that would set her free from any guilt and obligation to the drunken pact she'd made with Abby and Ruth.

Chapter Six

Henrietta slowed her pace as she neared the corner of Mulberry and Cross Street. The sun crested the tops of the surrounding buildings, providing extra light to guide her early morning journey. After turning onto Mulberry Street, her destination would be about twenty or so yards away. She pulled the rusted timepiece from the hidden pocket in the fold of her dress. She had ten minutes to spare. But when one was meeting with another in a congested area to conduct a covert exchange of sensitive information, it was better to arrive early rather than late.

She stopped on the corner and peered to the left, then right, surveying the crowded street. Men and women ambled along the sidewalks, some occasionally crossing to the other side. Young boys paraded along the dirt road, shouting the latest headline from the morning paper as they waved it in the air, hoping to entice a passerby to purchase a copy.

She made sure not to stare at anyone for too long. Her eyes flicked up, then back to the ground, repeating the action several times. Head bowed, she took a left onto Mulberry Street, keeping her pace unhurried and even.

She continued surveying her surroundings, her gaze darting up then down, taking in as much detail of what was happening as possible. Across the street from what she assumed was her destination, a carriage idled, its driver perched on the box, the reigns slung over his forearm as he picked dirt from beneath his nails. Like everyone else, he ignored her. No one paid attention to a hunched colored woman in a dull white head wrap and plain gray factory uniform, carrying a basket of vegetables closer to needing to be composted than consumed.

She strolled along, unnoticed as if she were a ghost. However, despite her outward appearance of composure, each step shredded her nerves like a cat dragging its claws along the delicate fabric of a silk evening gown. She concentrated on taking deep, steady breaths to ward off the suffocating grip of paranoia riding her hard.

"I want to join the Black Militia for Union Victory," she'd told her Uncle Paul. "I can help gather intelligence." The foolhardiness of those words pressed in on her from all sides. What she wouldn't give to turn back the clock and make sure they remained lodged in her throat. Then again, he hadn't been supposed to tell her, "yes."

At first, she hadn't believed him when he gave his consent during their walk after dinner Friday evening. But then the missive arrived Saturday morning, stating he had an assignment she could complete. She'd nearly keeled over reading the note and thought surely, she'd died and been sent to her eternal damnation.

Stopping in front of a shabby brick tenement building, she peered up at the black metal numbers above the door. This was it. Her contact should be here at any minute.

She assessed the area until she saw a woman leaning from an open window, hanging her freshly laundered clothes on a line. Before Henrietta could look away, the woman peered down at her. Deep-set brown eyes spread a bit too far apart on a golden, tan face regarded her with mild curiosity before focusing back on the laundry. Henrietta dropped her gaze back to the ground, cursing herself for being noticed. A shudder turned chill snaked down her spine, leaving a trail of gooseflesh in its wake. Each second under the woman's scrutiny had stopped, then started, her heart more times than she could count.

What was I thinking? She was a woman of means who spent her time as a volunteer schoolmarm for adults learning to read and write. She wasn't a spy. Blast and tarnation to Ruby and Abby for forcing her to uphold their pledge. How could she have allowed herself to be convinced that this was anything other than a dim-witted, ill-advised, horrendous idea?

On a Sunday morning, she was supposed to be lying in bed until her mother forced her to prepare for church, not slinking through the shadows of one of the most dangerous neighborhoods in New York City. She'd never drink another drop of alcohol until the end of her days if she made it through today unscathed.

The front door of the building opened and a slim man, sporting an equally slim mustache that curled at the ends, stepped into the early morning sun. She watched him bob down the steps, a faint rosy tint to his cheeks, and a whistle on his lips. Was this her contact? Uncle Paul hadn't given her a description of the man, and she'd been too shocked by his willingness to let her execute the meeting to ask for one.

Henrietta took a step forward then halted. The door to the building flung open again, emitting a stout, shapely woman holding a cloth sack. She jogged down the stairs shouting, "Wait, Peter. Your lunch."

The man turned, his cheeks and corners of his mouth lifting in a toothy grin. He held his arms wide and waited for her to reach him. The woman hardly slowed before crashing into him, then wrapped her arms around him in a tight embrace.

Henrietta's heart melted into a puddle of sappy emotion, then hardened, coated in a layer of envy. Images of a certain Irishman assailed her. To love and be loved so fully by Elijah was a dream she couldn't allow herself to entertain. To do so would be almost as foolish as standing outside a half-dilapidated building waiting for someone she'd never met.

Henrietta released a drawn-out breath. The Union would find a way to beat the Confederacy even without her assistance. She should return home and pretend that this moment of lunacy had never occurred.

She took one last long, hard look at the building. "Go home," the shrill voice of reason commanded. She adjusted the basket of vegetables from one arm to the other to alleviate the ache in her muscles and give herself time to produce arguments in favor of proceeding with this mission. None came to mind. Ready to give in, she examined the building a final time, then stepped backward. Then another. And another.

"The sky is rather blue today isn't it cadet?" a rich deep voice said from behind her.

A high pitched yelp sprang from Henrietta's mouth before she could stop it. Her grip tightened on the basket handle so tightly if it were a human neck, she'd find herself on trial for murder. She whirled around to face the person who frightened her soul from her.

The carriage driver stood before her, his expression composed and unreadable. Henrietta peered at the carriage, it's emptiness confirming the identity of the man before her, then at the people moving around them. Several pairs of eyes stared in their direction for a short time, before dismissing them and continuing on their way.

Henrietta looked back at the man in front of her. When had he left the carriage? When had he walked across the street? How had she not noticed? She released a humorless laugh. This was further proof that the life of a spy was not the one for her. The man stared at her, not saying a word as if waiting for... *Oh!* His words penetrated her befuddling haze of shock. *Blue sky. Cadet.* Those were the code words Uncle Paul had given her.

"It is Captain. Not a gray cloud in sight." She repeated the phrase her uncle had instructed her to use when she found her contact.

The driver nodded. A beam of sunlight reflected off the sweat covering the expanse of his shiny forehead left uncovered by his receding hairline. His expression wasn't friendly, but it wasn't hostile either.

"Shall we go then? I'll escort you to the East River ferry and you can relay your good news along the way."

He knew her route home? Of course, he did. Uncle Paul entrusted him with more information, than he apparently did her.

"Yes. Let us depart."

"Very well." He waved an arm before him, inviting her to proceed him to the carriage.

Holding her basket with both hands, she pulled it close to her chest. This was the end of her mission. She'd done it.

All that remained was extracting the information from her brain and relaying it to this man in a coherent manner. A sudden lightness washed over her. She stifled a satisfied grin, straightened her spine, and marched toward the carriage with her head held high.

Maybe she'd overreacted. Maybe she could do this. Maybe she could be an asset to the militia.

Elijah hurried down the hall, headed toward the stables to prepare the carriage. For the second time this week, a strange sight caught his attention when he passed the kitchen. He backpedaled, then stopped to examine the situation unfolding before him.

Henrietta cracked open the kitchen's back door barely wide enough for her to squeeze through, sneaking into the house wearing... He squinted to make sure his eyes didn't deceive him. Sure enough, she wore a ratty old faded apron over a dirty threadbare gray dress. She looked like a homeless beggar woman from Five Points.

Where on earth had she found that outfit? And why was she wearing it?

Elijah pressed his fist to his lips to keep from laughing aloud. Whatever she was up to, he had to keep watching this scenario to its conclusion. He stepped back, hiding behind the edge of the door frame, and craned his neck to peer back into the kitchen. Henrietta carefully closed the door with excruciating slowness, occasionally looking to her left, then right. She paused each time the door creaked, her entire body going still.

When the door was closed and bolted, she looked around once more. Thinking no one watched, she stuck her hand inside the basket dangling from her arm and rummaged around beneath the sparse offerings of vegetables. She pulled out a thin square piece of paper.

Elijah's frown deepened the longer he watched her. Sneaking in. Secret notes. He didn't know what she was up to, but he didn't like it. If this had anything to do with what she was bickering with Ruth and Abigail about, it couldn't be anything good.

He entered the kitchen. Leaning against the door frame, hands in his pockets he asked, "What are you up to?"

"Oh!" She jumped, her hand shooting to her chest, sending the piece of paper fluttering to the floor. She spun around her frumpy dress swishing about her ankles before her frantic gaze locked on him. Worry transformed into recognition, which transformed into annoyance across her beautiful tawny-brown face. "Elijah! Why you… You frightened me!"

Her voice dripped with enough malevolence to make a weaker man's backbone disintegrate. But he didn't mind the challenge burning in her eyes, daring him to feel anything other than remorse for his actions. Remorse, however, was the last thing he felt.

"I can see that." His suspicion grew the more her eyes narrowed on him. "But I would not have scared you if you weren't sneaking into the house. What are you up to? Did you go out begging for food?"

She crossed her arms over her chest. "How very witty of you."

"Thank you for noticing. But back to the original topic. Why are you sneaking into the house dressed in those clothes?"

"Not that it is any of your business," she said, then cleared her throat and smoothed her hands over her apron. Her gaze flicked around the room before landing back on him. "I wasn't feeling well and thought a bit of fresh air would go a long way toward returning me to full health. I do believe it worked, as I feel much better."

He lifted an eyebrow and scratched along his bearded jaw. For the past two years, he'd learned everything about her. Possibly more than she knew about herself. Like when she lied, the muscle above her right cheek ticked, as it did now.

"You mean to tell me you went for a walk in that dress?" He jutted his chin in her direction. "How daft do you think I am? What were you really doing?"

Henrietta tossed aside the basket of rotting vegetables and placed her fists on her hips. "What I've done with my morning is none of your concern."

"What will your mother think of you sneaking about looking like a common pauper?"

His words hit their mark. She took a small step back, her expression filled with dread, like a wounded animal facing a dangerous foe. Henrietta sought her mother's approval in everything she did. Whatever this little charade was, they both knew her mother wouldn't be pleased with it. Perhaps if he couldn't convince her with common sense to stay away from whatever foolishness she was engaged in, threatening to tell her mother would do the trick.

"You wouldn't dare."

Elijah took a step forward, erasing the distance between them. He lowered his voice to a menacing whisper. "Wouldn't I?"

Henrietta's mouth opened, then closed. He could see the calculation in her eyes as she debated whether or not his threat was genuine. It very much so was.

"My father died six years ago, and I don't need another. What will your silence cost me?"

"The truth."

"I can't give that to you."

"Then a promise that you won't do anything dangerous."

"I can't give you that, either."

"Henrietta..."

She raised her hands in surrender. "But I can say it is not your place to worry about me. I can't stop you from telling my mother, but I hope that you won't. If you do, I will deny it, and you will forever have lost my confidence. Now if you will excuse me, I need to prepare for church."

Henrietta gathered the skirt of her tattered dress and sashayed out of the kitchen with all the grace and dignity of a woman wearing the finest silks and satins. Elijah ground his teeth; his hands fisted at his sides while he watched her leave. He'd done a fine job handling this situation.

His plan to convince her to stay safe had gone terribly wrong. He'd finally had a chance to be bold and talk to her about something other than what chores she needed doing, and he'd ruined it. Shoving his hands in his pockets, his mood officially soured, he left the kitchen and marched the rest of the way to the stables with a dark cloud hovering over him.

Chapter Seven

Henrietta closed her eyes, reveling in the melodic harmony of the congregation as they sang her favorite hymn. The only things that got her out of bed and into the cramped church pews every Sunday were a potential tongue-lashing from her mother and the beautiful songs. Especially on oppressive summer days like today, which made it easy to imagine the devil was indeed alive.

A bony elbow to her ribs interrupted the lulling trance of the song. Henrietta peeked at Abby and Ruth standing beside her. Matching amused conspiratorial smirks graced their lips. What on earth were these two up to now?

Neither enjoyed any part of the church service, not even the hymns. Hence why they had no issue being inattentive and finding creative ways to entertain themselves while passing the time. Abby, as one of the few non-colored people in the building, only came to spend time with Henrietta and Ruth. Her parents weren't particularly religious and didn't adhere to the social construct mandating church to be part of a person's weekly schedule. Ruth only came to add to her repository of favors Henrietta owed her for being such a wonderful friend. Either way, Henrietta was pleased each time they showed up and marched into the pew like two prisoners headed to the gallows.

Keeping her hand low near her stomach, Abby pointed to the scene unfolding four pews in front of them on the left side of the aisle. Her white-gloved hand pressed against her lips blocking her tittering from spilling forth. Following the direction of Abby's finger, Henrietta caught sight of Mrs. Wilson slouching in her chair, her arms and head draped over the back of the wooden bench. Four other women beat their fans against the air, whipping up a small breeze that made the plethora of flowers and feathers in her bonnet dance to the rhythm they set. The feathers bent backward then stood erect, repeating the motions in time with the wind. Starting then stopping when the women's arms grew tired.

Henrietta sucked in her lips to contain her laugh at the overly dramatic display. Yes, it was hot, but if Mrs. Wilson didn't come to church in the middle of summer wearing a high-neck dress with skirts made of unnecessary voluminous yards of fabric, crinolines, and hoops all for the sake of fashion, she wouldn't be facing near heat-induced death.

Like many of the members of the congregation, status and reputation meant everything to Mrs. Wilson. Middle-class free colored people who'd carved a little piece of wealth for themselves from the harsh American landscape needed everyone to know. Especially now as the states battled over the issue of slavery and the humanity of the African people.

Ruth leaned over Abigail and whispered, "The old bird is going to melt into a puddle of her own foolish vanity. She looks ridiculous in that dress, but I must admit this is the most exciting thing that's happened thus far. I'm grateful the Lord deemed it right to deliver such a humorous moment to us heathens."

Henrietta leaned closer to her friends, shaking her head. "You know how these ladies are. Promise me that if I ever become more concerned with status than common sense, you will drag me out back and hogtie me to a tree until I'm a rational human being again."

The three of them muffled their laughter behind their hands but couldn't contain every noise resulting from their chortling. A collective shush rose from the pew in front of them. Henrietta and Abby cast their eyes to the floor, having the good sense to don a demure, regretful countenance. Ruth, on the other hand, stared the group of sour-faced old women down until they turned around with a collective huff.

Great. No doubt Mother would hear about this incident at the end of service and the entire journey home, Henrietta would receive an earful about her need to be more respectful to the elderly, and a woman's duty to be couth and above reproach at all times.

As if to prove her assumption correct, her mother looked over her shoulder, leveling a questioning eyebrow at Henrietta from the first pew. Dang it all. Henrietta tucked her chin to her chest, her head bent in a sorrowful pose, and folded her hands in front of her chest as if she were praying for mercy. Silently, she was.

Her mother faced forward, shaking her head, and continued singing. Lancing her friends with a chastening glare, Henrietta brought a finger to her lips to denote the end to their misbehavior. Abby and Ruth faced forward, pretending to be engrossed in the hymn until the singing came to an end.

"Everyone may be seated," the preacher said. He moseyed to the podium with a Bible tucked under his arm.

Henrietta took her seat along with the rest of the congregation. She tried to focus on the preacher, but the hairs along her arms stood on end, and a familiar pull beckoned for her to heed it. Like a dying man in a desert, unable to resist the call of a shaded oasis, her gaze traveled to Elijah sitting next to her mother.

He shook his head, an amused grin conveying his enjoyment of her impropriety. Hopefully, that meant he'd forgiven her for her rude behavior early that morning. Normally, she'd never speak to him in such a manner. Being caught and then questioned about her foray into the world of clandestine operations had thrown her off. Either way, she'd have to make it a point later to apologize for her disrespectful tone.

She mustered a small smile for him, afraid anything more would give away the fact that her heart taped a quickened beat just from looking at him. She had to press a hand to her stomach to control the swarm of flutters his lingering gaze unleashed in her.

"Now, back to our discussion," Ruth whispered, leaning over Abby as if her brain had already disposed of the memory of being chastised.

Henrietta glanced at Ruth, then back at Elijah, but he'd already turned around. She could never hold a grudge against her friend, especially for something as trivial as interrupting her moment with Elijah. But she'd be a liar if she said she hadn't wished Ruth had better timing.

"I'd never let you become one of these stuffy old biddies. Starting with helping you come to your senses about your choice of husband."

That caught Henrietta's attention. She turned to Ruth, her eyebrows scrunched together, and her head shaking slowly. "What on earth are you talking about?"

Ruth tilted her head to the side and pursed her lips, a "don't be daft" expression on her face. She turned her head, and Henrietta followed her line of sight to the row of people in the first pew. It wasn't hard to decipher who she meant. Besides Abby, Elijah was the only other non-colored person in the room, making him the inappropriate choice and thus the one Ruth championed.

"I know who I should marry," Henrietta whispered back. She fidgeted in her chair, dusting her hands over the skirt of her dress to remove the imaginary specks of lint. "Your assistance is not needed in the matters of my matrimonial decisions."

Ruth opened her mouth to respond then closed it, her countenance souring when something at the back of the church caught her attention. Henrietta turned to see the source of her displeasure. Matthew strolled through the door, all unapologetic charm as if he hadn't arrived thirty minutes late to service.

Henrietta shook her head, balling the fabric of her dress in her tight fists. She and Matthew had discussed his tardiness many times, and after each discussion, he'd apologize and then swear he would change, but he never did. Tardiness for any social function got the gaggle of noisy busybodies talking mercilessly about the offender. And make no mistake, church was a social function.

Matthew promenaded down the aisle, smiling and waving at people as he passed. Henrietta cringed on the inside. First, he came in late; now he drew attention to himself. The

why she forced them to stand there and listen to this prattle never made sense to Henrietta.

Elijah couldn't come around with the carriage soon enough. Like she did every Sunday, Henrietta counted the seconds until he arrived. For that one thing, she admitted to herself that he was her knight in shining armor.

"Good morning, Mrs. Miller, my dearest sister-in-law, Henrietta," her Uncle Paul said, as he strolled up to their little group. Despite talking to all of them, he looked straight at Henrietta.

"Good morning," they all replied.

He tipped his hat to the older women in an easygoing manner and tucked his cane under his arm. That had to be a good sign. Didn't it? If she'd failed his test, his posture wouldn't be so relaxed. Henrietta's mood lightened as if a cloud had taken up residence in her heart. Hopefulness bubbled inside her until it was becoming nearly impossible for her to refrain from peppering him with questions in front of her mother and Mrs. Miller.

"I hate to interrupt your conversation rudely, but may I speak privately with Henrietta for a moment?"

"Of course, brother." Her mother said in a pleasant tone, then shooed them away.

"Thank you." He leaned in and kissed her mother on the cheek, then straightened and tipped his hat to Mrs. Miller. "You ladies have a wonderful rest of your day."

"You as well," both women replied.

Uncle Paul extended his crooked elbow, which Henrietta gladly accepted. They ambled away from the church in silence. As soon as they were close to the tree line surrounding the church and what Henrietta presumed was a good distance away from listening ears, her questions tumbled forth in rapid succession.

"Did I pass your test? Did I get in? Am I a member of the Black Militia for Union Victory? What will my duties be?"

Uncle Paul graced Henrietta with a wide grin. "My associate got back to me last night. He said you did a wonderful job. The message was correct, and you even took it upon yourself to dress the part."

The amused twinkle in his eyes, and praise of her job well done, made Henrietta feel invincible. She was going to play a part, no matter how small, in the victory she knew the Union would achieve at the end of this war. To think she'd been hesitant to participate and doubted her abilities to make a difference.

"We will discuss your duties on Wednesday. I will be at your house around three to retrieve you. And I'll take you to meet the other members of the militia."

"Excellent. And if I may, I'd like to inform you that I can decipher codes. It is a skill someone taught me years ago, and I've been increasing my proficiency in the art ever since."

"Intriguing. That skill is always needed in times of war. I will let the other members know, and you may show us what you can do on Wednesday."

"Wonderful." Henrietta stopped walking, forcing her uncle to do the same. Facing him, she took both his hands in hers and tried to convey her gratitude. "Thank you, Uncle. I didn't know how much this would mean to me, but I cherish this opportunity more than words can express. I won't let you down."

His expression warm and confident, he patted the top of Henrietta's hands, then gave them a gentle squeeze. "I know you won't. I have nothing but complete confidence in you."

Hearing those words from him thrummed on Henrietta's heartstrings. It was almost as if she were hearing them from her father. Pride and excitement infused her smile, filling it with a special joy she hadn't experienced since her father's death. For her country, for her people, for her father, and for herself, she would be the best member the Black Militia for Union Victory ever had.

Chapter Eight

Elijah peered up at the early morning sky. Birds stretched their wings and glided across the crystal blue expanse with the ease and grace of creatures that had not a care in the world. He'd give anything to have even a fraction of their freedom someday. But that was not the way life worked. Except for the lucky few, exempt from its harsh sting, life handed out struggles that everyone had to survive until the good Lord called them home.

The birds made a great juxtaposition to many of the men in the city below them. A solemn, almost hollow mood blanketed the usually lively and bustling New York City streets. The first draft had taken place a little less than two days ago.

Many men had found out if they would be forced to fight for their country. Elijah understood the need for more bodies for the war effort, but that didn't make him like it. He couldn't imagine being forced to march off to some battlefield for the purpose of courting death. After waking up this morning, he'd said a special prayer for the men whose names had been called.

Elijah sat in the driver's seat of the carriage swaying to its bumpy rhythm as the horses trotted down the street. Maybe it was his imagination, but there seemed to be fewer people around than usual. A scant number of individuals moseyed down the streets, dashing in and out of shops. He tipped his hat to a couple as he passed and received lukewarm smiles in return.

He didn't blame them. If it weren't for Henrietta needing him to bring her to the Colored Orphanage, he wouldn't be out and about. He'd spend the day in silent reflection at home, being grateful his name wasn't called.

Elijah guided the carriage onto Fifth Avenue, then pulled on the reins slowing the horses' pace when they neared their destination. The withering void of melancholy consuming him ebbed away when they stopped in front of the three-story building that housed hundreds of orphaned colored children. Henrietta had asked him to bring her here several times over the years. On occasion, he'd accompany her into the building to assist with any repairs requested by the matrons who ran the institution.

Each time he came, the children stole another piece of his heart. He'd never claim to know what it was like to be in their shoes, but he could appreciate and understand the strength it took each of them to continue to laugh, love, and thirst for education and a better life, despite their circumstances. It was too bad he had to run a few errands and couldn't come in today. He secured the reins, then hopped down from the driver's seat and opened the carriage door.

"Thank you," Henrietta said, gently placing her hand in his for him to help her step down.

The warmth of her heated skin seeped through her glove, adding fuel to the ever-smoldering passionate flame that burned inside him only for her. Elijah stroked his thumb over her knuckles, needing the added connection. Henrietta's lips parted, and her gaze jumped to his, but she didn't pull away. For a moment, they stood on the street, eyes locked, lost in a place where only the two of them existed.

"I'm sorry," Henrietta blurted out, breaking the trance.

"For what?"

She withdrew her hand from his. Her lashes fluttered down, blocking her sorrowful deep brown eyes from his view. "The way I spoke to you yesterday. When you scared me, I let my emotions get the better of me and my tongue. I said things that were rude, and that I didn't mean. Can you forgive me?"

Elijah lifted her chin, bringing her gaze back to his. "I forgave you the second it was over. But I do hope I have enough of your confidence that you can tell me what you were up to. I only want you to be safe."

"I know. And it's not that I don't trust you, but I can't tell you what I was doing because it is greater than just me. I will say it was important, and you have nothing to worry about."

No matter what she said, he'd always worry about her. The world was generally was not a kind place. But he couldn't expect her to cower at home, refusing to live her life or take part in things she believed in because there might be a little danger. That was not truly living. Besides, he wasn't her husband or anyone of significance in her life. He was in her employ. He had no right to ask anything of her.

Elijah ran a finger along her cheek, then took a step back and shoved his hands in his pockets. "Apologies. I overstepped my boundaries, madam. You're right to refuse to confide in the hired help. Please excuse the slip."

"Elijah, I don't mind..."

"What time should I pick you up?"

She reached out, then let her hand drop, as if thinking better of touching him. Elijah was both relieved and disappointed. The lines of their relationship had begun to blur over the last week. He needed to remember that she was the beautiful woman whose family paid his salary, and he'd never be worthy of such a blessing.

"I should be ready to depart around three."

"I will be waiting for you out front at a quarter till."

"Thank you."

Elijah turned his back on Henrietta, and the impossible things she made him want then trudged back to the carriage. He needed a drink. A stiff one. Since he didn't have to collect Henrietta until three, he had more than enough time to make a stop after his errands. And he knew just the place to go.

Six eggs or five? Or was it three? Henrietta's hand hovered over the brown shells of the item in question, frozen in indecision. She couldn't remember how many eggs a basic cake recipe required. Baking had never been a talent she'd possessed, but when Anna-Beth had tugged on her skirt and proudly announced it was her birthday, Henrietta couldn't resist the little girl's request for a cake to celebrate the occasion.

Now if she could only recall the ingredients necessary to make one. She'd hurried off to the grocery nearly thirty minutes ago and was no closer to knowing what she needed now than when she arrived.

"Excuse me, madam," Henrietta said to the young woman standing next to the flour, finally giving in and asking for help. "Would you happen to know how..."

Henrietta's question trailed off when a loud crashing noise outside the shop caught her attention. A new sound emerged on the tail end of the last. Was that... screaming? Curiosity made her want to go to the window and investigate. Instinct kept her frozen in place, staring at the woman she'd been talking to.

"There's one in here. She's a fancy Negro too."

Henrietta's attention snapped to the man holding the shop door open, pointing an accusatory finger at her. She took a small step back. Then another. And another, until her hip connected with the sharp wooden corner of a produce table. Apples tumbled to the floor, thudding around her feet, but Henrietta couldn't tear her eyes off the man and the small crowd gathering around him.

Their intense, fevered stares hammered the sharp spikes of terror deep into her heart. They stalked into the store, faces tight, and skin stretched into loathsome snarls. Never in her life had Henrietta ever witnessed so much hatred directed at her. These people loathed her very existence and wanted to wipe her off the face of the earth.

"Help," Henrietta pleaded in a choked voice. "Please help me."

Banishing enough of her terror to take control of her motor functions, she scrambled back, her gaze bouncing between the other patrons in the store.

"Please, help me," Henrietta pleaded again, her voice stronger.

No one moved to assist her. They moved away, allowing the small group unobstructed access to her. Many averted their eyes, their heads hanging in shame and guilt, but not enough to risk their safety for hers.

"Le-e-leave her alone," the shopkeeper piped up in a weak voice.

"Shut up, old man. This don't concern you."

The shopkeeper didn't say another word. He dropped his eyes to the ground and became a mute statue, like everyone else in the store.

Tears stung the back of Henrietta's eyes. What was happening? What was the meaning of this? She glanced out the window, and like something out of a nightmare, a mob of people had taken to the city streets, rioting and destroying everything they came in contact with. Negro men, women, and children fled from attackers swinging clubs, tossing bricks, and kicking and punching anyone with brown skin.

"Get her," the ringleader growled, jutting his chin in Henrietta's direction.

The men darted forward; their hands curled like claws ready to lay claim to their prey. Henrietta dropped her basket of groceries and frantically searched for an escape but found none. There were too many of them, and they all blocked the store's sole exit.

She dodged to the left when someone tried to grab her, but it was no use. Thick fingers bit into her shoulder so hard that she would have crumbled under the pain if they weren't holding her in place.

A bony hand shot out, striking her across the face. "Stupid whore," one of her attackers hissed. "You think you're better than us with your fancy dress and jewelry, don't you? You're not. You're probably some white man's bed wench. Well, we work hard for everything we have, and you and your dirty kin ain't going to take it from us. We'll show you what happens to Negros who think higher of themselves than they ought."

A round of cheers erupted from Henrietta's attackers. Tears welled in her eyes, blurring her vision and making it difficult to see clearly. Someone tugged on the sleeve of her dress, ripping the delicate fabric.

The burn of her hair being ripped from her scalp soon joined the sting in her cheek when someone yanked her head back, exposing the tender flesh of her neck. Her heart completely stopped when the cool metal of a sharp blade pressed into her neck.

Oh, God. These people meant to kill her. She wrapped her arms around her middle, wishing she could curl up into a tiny ball until this miserable torment ended.

"Please," she begged in a watery voice. "Please let me go. Please."

"The stupid wench thinks we care about her pleading," one of the men said, sending them all into a round of snickering. "Guess I'll have to show her how much we don't."

A meaty hand dipped into the front of Henrietta's bodice and tore the front of her dress. The blade lowered from her throat, then sliced across the top of the soft flesh of her bosom. She gritted her teeth and stomped her foot, trying to dispel the pain and keep from giving them the satisfaction of hearing her cry out. Pressure built in her head from holding her breath to contain her scream until white spots began to dot her vision. Unable to contain it any longer, Henrietta's shrill, high-pitched shriek pierced the air.

"Get your fecking hands off her, you bunch of dirty growlers, else I'll give ye a clatter in the jaw," a familiar voice snarled in a heavy Irish accent.

The sting of the knife sliding across Henrietta's skin suddenly disappeared. A new flood of tears welled in Henrietta's eyes for an entirely different reason.

"Who the hell are you?" asked the ringleader.

Deep, black, sinister hatred like nothing he'd ever felt before consumed Elijah. The moment he'd walked into the store and saw Henrietta in those men's hands, all he'd wanted was to kill every single one of them. Her agonizing screams awakened a murderous beast he didn't know lived inside him.

Who was he? He'd show them who he was.

The crunch of breaking bones when his fist connected with a fat, bulbous nose was the only response Elijah gave to the question of his identity. He was the man that would deliver pain like nothing these ratbags had ever known. The retched scoundrel howled in pain and grabbed his nose to try to steam the blood pouring between his fingers. Elijah could smell the stench of fear and uncertainty emanating from the screaming man's comrades.

"How dare you put your hands on her," he seethed, his near-crazed gaze dropping to the two pairs of hands still holding on to Henrietta's arms.

The cowards released her, snatching back their hands as if she'd suddenly combusted into a scorching ball of fire. Henrietta crumpled to the floor, her entire body shaking.

Dead. They were all dead.

Elijah lashed out, his fists punching and connecting with whatever part of the men he could reach. Blind rage crept from the edge of his consciousness, stifling his sanity until the only thing he was capable of doing was delivering blow after bone-crushing blow.

At some point, a knife ended up in his hand. He was cognizant of his arm slashing over and over, but it didn't feel like it was him doing the action. It was as if he'd left his body and given it over to a spirit of vengeance.

"Elijah, stop, please. Take me home. I want to go home."

Henrietta's soft voice broke through Elijah's violent haze, releasing him from his avenging trance. He blinked several times, then looked down at his blood-soaked hands. A few cuts crisscrossed his arms and hands, but most of the blood didn't belong to him. The four men who attacked Henrietta were sprawled out across the floor, closer to death than life.

Elijah threw the knife down, then ran over and scooped Henrietta into his arms. He adjusted the torn fabric of her bodice and used it to apply pressure to her wound. "Hold this here to stunt the bleeding," he told Henrietta, taking her hand and placing it on the fabric over her injury.

Cradling her his arms like a fragile piece of glass, he stood and barreled out of the store. "I'm so sorry," he whispered into her hair. "I'm so, so sorry."

Henrietta didn't reply. She nestled closer to his chest, her delicate hand fisting the fabric of his shirt like it was the only thing keeping her from shattering. Elijah tightened his hold on her, blocking her from the chaos surrounding them.

In a matter of hours, a handful of New York City citizens had relinquished their humanity and begun looting, rioting, and attacking colored men, women, and children. It sickened him to see the devastation and destruction being carried out, but as much as he wanted to help, Henrietta was his top priority. He had to get her home to safety.

She was all that mattered.

Chapter Nine

"This is why I need to enlist."

Thomas's infuriated voice greeted Henrietta when she awakened from a sleep that she didn't remember succumbing to. The last thing she recalled was going to buy ingredients for Anna-Beth's cake, then... Then four men attached her

And Elijah had saved her.

Elijah.

She scraped the bottom of the barrel of her energy reserves and peeled open an eye. She did a quick sweep of the room before her strength fled, and she closed it back. Elijah wasn't here. Only her Uncle Paul, sitting in a chair in the corner of her bedroom attempting to read a newspaper while Thomas paced in front of him.

Her cousin cracked his knuckles as if trying to defuse some of the tension cording his muscles beneath his skin.

"We need to fight back," Thomas said, slamming his fist into his palm. "That's the only way we'll see real change. Not even having money can save us from those animals. We need to show we aren't afraid of them, and we will no longer take their abuse."

"They aren't animals. They are scared men with families they can barely feed. They fear the freeing of slaves because they believe it will mean more competition for already scarce jobs." Uncle Paul kept his voice neutral, but Henrietta could hear the impatience skirting the edge of his tone.

"And that gives them the right to attack us? To burn us in the streets?"

"No, it doesn't. But it also doesn't give us permission to emulate their fits of violence. Especially not in my household. We are better than that."

"Father, I..."

"Be quiet, Thomas," Henrietta croaked through dry lips. She'd heard enough, and the throbbing in her head intensified with each decibel his voice rose. She rolled onto her side, then pried her eyes open and peered at him.

"Hating them like they hate us makes you no better than them."

"Go fetch your aunt," Uncle Paul commanded before Thomas could reply.

Thomas stayed rooted in place for a few defiant moments. His flaring nostrils and wide, domineering stance made it clear he had plenty more to say on the topic of his enlistment, but thankfully, he let it go.

"Yes, sir. Glad to see you awake, cousin." Thomas dipped his head, then stalked off.

When he was out of the room, Henrietta gave into her weariness, and let her eyes droop, but fought to keep them open.

Uncle Paul rose from his chair, then walked across the room and perched on the edge of her bed. He patted her hand resting on the mattress. "How are you feeling, my dear?"

"Like an angry mob of men tried to wrench my head from my neck then slice my chest open. Oh, wait. They did."

Henrietta smiled at her uncle and her self-deprecating joke. To her surprise, he didn't share in her amusement. Instead, he averted his gaze, a solemnness settling over him.

"When Elijah..." The rest of his sentence clogged in his throat. He sat a little taller and adjusted the lapels of his coat. He swallowed hard, making his Adam's apple bob, then tried again. "When Elijah carried you into the house covered in blood and unconscious, something hit me. You're my brother's only child. My last connection to him. I can't lose you and I can't put you in harm's way. I'm sorry, but I can't allow you to join the militia."

Henrietta's chest seized, panic embedding itself deep in her heart. He couldn't deny her now, not after what happened to her. Now more than ever, she needed to play a role in bringing about the Union victory. To give her people an opportunity to pursue a life on their own terms, with the power of the law finally on their side.

She gripped her uncle's forearms with trembling hands. "No, Uncle. I have to join. I *will* join."

"I'm sorry, but no. It wasn't real, anyway. The test was a controlled situation, with a man I trusted with my life. You were in no real danger. I figured having you by my side where I can keep an eye on you would be better than you pestering me endlessly like Thomas. I planned to give you fake assignments, but now I can no longer even pretend to allow you to be near harm."

He pried her hands from his arms, then gave them a subdued pat, unable to make eye contact

G.S. CARR

with her. No. He couldn't do this to her. He couldn't deny her this now that she wanted it so badly. But there would be no use arguing with him. His mind was made up and whining and pleading wouldn't change it. She had to show him she was an invaluable asset no matter the risk.

"I understand, Uncle. Please excuse my impertinence."

"There is nothing to forgive. I will let you rest. Your mother should be in soon to check on you."

"Thank you."

Henrietta didn't stop her uncle when he stood, then moved to exit the room. She understood his concern. If their roles were reversed, she'd probably feel the same way. Nevertheless, she wouldn't let him stop her. She'd prove herself, and she knew exactly how she'd do it.

As if sensing his need to be rescued, her mother swept into the room and rushed to Henrietta's bedside. "Thank heavens that you're finally awake. The doctor said you'd recover quickly, but you were asleep for two days. I was so worried."

Her puffy red eyes made it easy for Henrietta to guess *worried* was a mild way to describe

106

what her mother had been feeling. And she'd been sleeping for two days? Her body must have been in worse shape than she realized.

"It's all right, Mother. I will survive." She did her best to give her mother a reassuring smile, but if it was half as droopy as her eyelids, she missed the mark. Talking with her uncle had siphoned most of her energy.

"I know you will."

Henrietta closed her eyes and enjoyed the caress of her mother's soft fingers brushing the hair back from her forehead. No matter how old she got, she'd never get enough of her mother fussing over her.

She lay still when her mother pulled the blanket up to her chin, then tucked it around her shoulders. Her mother kissed her again, then ran a hand down her back as if needing constant contact with Henrietta to reassure herself all was well.

"Oh. Before I forget, there is someone who'd like to see you."

Henrietta's eyes wrenched open and flicked to the door. Finally, Elijah had come to visit her. She'd been surprised that he wasn't there when she woke.

"Come in, dear," her mother called, raising her voice.

Henrietta's heart sunk when her visitor strolled through the door. A heavy weariness took hold of her body again, ten times worse than before. Matthew rushed to her bedside, an expression he thought conveyed concern etched across his face. Henrietta could sense the falseness of it. Yes, he was probably genuinely concerned that if something befell her, he would no longer have the rich bride whom he was counting on to fill his family's coffers.

But he wasn't genuinely concerned about *her*.

"Oh, my dearest sunflower." He sat on the other side of the bed, opposite her mother, then clutched her hand so tightly it hurt. "It is so good to see you well. I was so worried. You've been asleep for two days, but I've been here every day, waiting for you to wake."

"Yes, he has," her mother chimed in, with an enthusiastic nod of her head.

"Thank you for your concern, Matthew."

Her mother looked at Henrietta expectantly. This was the part where she was supposed to fall at his feet with gratitude that he would take the time out of his full schedule to visit her. Tossing in a flutter of her lashes and senseless giggle would go a long way toward stroking his ego as well. Unfortunately for both of them, she didn't have the strength nor desire to pretend she was glad to see him. It was interesting how being so close to death could do that to a person.

"If you both would excuse me, I would like to rest now. Thank you again, Matthew, for visiting. I'm sure my mother will keep you informed about my progress and let you know when I am feeling more up to having visitors, so you don't have to waste time coming to see me."

The smile teetered on his lips. "Yes, well, I know your ordeal took a lot out of you." He released her hand, then stood. Rubbing the back of his neck, he spoke without looking at her, "Rest up, and I will come back when you are feeling better."

"Thank you."

Matthew stiffly bent at the waist in a brusque bow to her, then her mother. "Have a lovely rest of your day Mrs. Wright."

"You as well, Matthew." Her mother gave him a strained smile, embarrassment painting her cheeks a faint shade of pink.

A charged silence filled the room while Henrietta and her mother waited for Matthew to leave. As soon as he stepped through the door, Henrietta began a countdown.

Four. Three. Two. One.

"Henrietta! That was impolite and rude. He came to spend time with you, and that's how you treat him? He's been courting you for over two years, and you're still dragging your feet on accepting his proposal. Any other man would have moved on to more eager pastures by now. You're lucky he still pays you any mind. What has gotten into you?"

Henrietta mentally rolled her eyes. She could point out the fact that Matthew would never pass up the opportunity to get his hands on their family's wealth no matter how eager other pastures were. Or that she knew he hadn't been a chaste monk abstaining from the pleasures of the flesh over the past two years of their courtship. So, it wasn't like he was desperately waiting for her to give him something he'd been missing.

Although, she could point all these things out and more, Henrietta refrained. There was no point taking out her surly mood on her mother. And she didn't wish to argue.

"I'm sorry, Mother, I don't know what's come over me. I will call on him when I am feeling better and make sure to thank him properly for his visits."

"Good."

Satisfied with Henrietta's answer, her mother went back to fussing over her. She tucked the covers around her again, then wiped a damp cloth over her warm skin.

Henrietta closed her eyes and tried to rest. She hadn't been completely honest with her mother. She knew why she'd given Matthew such a cold reception. The reason had flaming red hair, blue eyes, and strong arms that made her feel like nothing in the world could harm her when they were wrapped around her. Waking up without him by her side annoyed her more than she cared to admit. And she'd never confess such a thing to her mother. Thankfully, she didn't have long to wait before sleep claimed her once again.

Hands. So many hands clawed at Henrietta's dress, yanking and tossing her about like an unanchored ship on a violent ocean. She wrestled against their hold, but there were too many of them. Pale, dirt-smudged faces emerged from the darkness around her, their expressions pure rage and hatred.

Help. Help. She wanted to scream the word, but her mouth wouldn't cooperate. Wouldn't say the one word that would bring an end to her torment. Raw, searing pain sliced across the top of her bosom. She choked on the scream that refused to finish its climb up her windpipe. *Help. Please help. Help me, please.*

"Wake up. Wake up, *a stór*. Please wake up."

That voice. She knew that voice. Henrietta turned her head in the direction she heard it coming from. It came from somewhere close, yet far away. The angry faces faded, driven away by the voice.

Wait. This wasn't real.

Henrietta opened her eyes. She nearly wept at the sight that greeted her. "Elijah?"

"You're safe, *a stór*," he crooned in a soothing tone. "I've got you. It was just a nightmare."

Elijah sat next to her, his big body hunched so he could reach down and wipe the tears from her eyes. He'd come.

Henrietta glanced out the window. Stars glowed brightly in the coal-black night sky, accompanied by a round, full moon. It must be well into the night. Was this why he wasn't there when she'd awakened the first time? Because he came to visit her in the evening when everyone else had gone to sleep?

Ignoring the pain in her chest, she launched herself at him and folded her arms around his neck. She clung to him, needing to feel the safety and security he provided.

"Thank you. Thank you. Thank you." All she could do for a moment was repeat her gratitude, her voice filled with reverence. "Thank you so much for saving my life."

Elijah leaned back and lifted her chin so that their eyes met. "What did I tell you before? Never thank me for treating you the way I should. I'll save you every time you're in trouble, but it won't often happen because I swear to you, I'll do a better job of protecting you from here on."

"And I'll always show my appreciation for all that you do for me." Henrietta laid her head on his chest. Her unfocused eyes stared into the darkness around them, listening to the even rhythm of his heart. "What happened?"

His chest expanded, then sunk beneath her ear. The warm gust of his weary sigh tickled the hairs on the back of her neck.

"Men took to the streets to protest the lottery. At some point, it turned into violence and destruction of government property. Then they..." He scrubbed a hand over his face, taking a moment to compose himself. "Then they started attacking colored people. Men, women, and children, walking around not bothering anyone. They looted and burned homes and businesses. Anything in their path, they destroyed."

Henrietta squeezed her eyes shut against the images of defenseless people being assaulted and driven from the places they'd once felt safe. "When did it end?"

"It hasn't. Colored people are fleeing the city to find safety as we speak. Your mother and uncle have been working with neighbors and organizations to help wherever they can."

Elijah rubbed her back with slow, tender strokes. Could he feel the crushing sadness weighing on her heart? Her need to be comforted. She stiffened, withdrawing from his embrace when a thought struck her. She searched his face, needing to see the truth when he replied to her next question.

"The children at the orphanage. How are they?"

"The orphanage was attacked. Though none of the children were hurt," he added quickly. "The staff got them to the Thirty-Fifth Street police station, and they've been safe there ever since."

She covered her mouth with her hand and slumped back into his arms. "Good. Good," she said around shaky laughter. "And the building? Did it survive?"

He hung his head, staring at the bed as he shook it. "No. The looters picked it clean, then burned it. I'm sorry."

"No matter. The children are safe, and that's what's most important. We can rebuild the institution later."

Elijah's muscled bunched, and his arms tightened around her. "They should all be hanged, the entire lot of them."

Henrietta's stomach squeezed and bottomed out. She hugged her middle, shrinking into herself to ward off the eerie chill that suddenly sapped all the warmth from her body. Elijah's voice dripping with malice and loathing rang in her ears, sounding too similar to her attackers for Henrietta's liking.

"No. I don't condone what they've done, but I understand. Many of those people survived circumstances I could never imagine. Your people came here because of a famine that forced them to watch their loved ones starve to death. They came to America in search of a better life but were met with contempt and abuse. Now, they fear what the emancipation of all slaves will do to the little financial security they've managed to scrounge for themselves. They need to answer for what they've done because all actions have consequences, but it can't be done out of hateful spite."

A moment of silence fell over them. Elijah started rubbing her back again. "How are you the one turning me from my anger against my own people?"

Henrietta laughed softly, her head once again resting over his heart. "Because it is the right thing to do. Besides, you are only angry with them because they harmed me."

"Damn right, I am. They hurt you, *a stór*, and for that, I'd gladly rip each one of their heads from their feeble necks."

A stór. He'd called her that several times now. What did it mean? Henrietta made a mental note to ask him once their current line of conversation came to an end.

"Well, now you must forgive as I have done. We need to focus on rebuilding, not continuing the destruction. Besides, I don't want you stewing on it when I take you on a picnic." Her last sentence had not been planned, but as soon as it sprang into her head, she knew she had to say it.

Elijah's hand froze in the middle of her back. "A picnic? For what?"

"To say thank you."

"You don't have to."

"I know. I want to. Now, stop arguing with me and tell me a story."

Yes, she was changing the subject, but she didn't know what else to do. The longer she thought about enjoying an amicable social outing with Elijah, the more she wanted it to happen and wouldn't take no for an answer.

"A story?"

"Yes, any you'd like. One from your country, perhaps. My strength is waning again, but I'm not ready to be alone to yet."

"As you wish, *a stór*. I think I know the perfect one."

Henrietta nestled further into his arms until she found a comfortable position that she could lie in for however long he decided to stay. Hopefully, it would be until she fell asleep. She wasn't ready to be alone just yet. Or without the comforting security that she felt enveloped in his embrace.

Chapter Ten

Winter rain falls through the night. Farewell, my darling rider.

Henrietta finished the sentence with an elegant swirl on the last letter, then stabbed the paper to add a bold period that slightly bled through the paper. Placing her pen on the desk, she lifted the page and stared down at her handiwork. She took a deep satisfied breath, expanding her lungs to their fullest capacity. This had to be one of her best ciphers yet. It never ceased to amaze her every time she crafted a message hidden beneath another string of words.

She scanned the letter one last time.

Perfection. She dusted the letter then folded it. A knock sounded on her bedroom door right before she placed the note in an envelope.

"Yes?" Henrietta called through her closed door.

"It's me, ma'am. Nancy. Ms. Ruth and Ms. Abigail are here to see you. They told me to tell you to come down quickly. Your mother told them you awoke last night, and they've been dying to see you since they heard what happened, so don't keep them waiting."

"That sounds like them," Henrietta said, her voice tinged with amusement. "Give me a moment."

Henrietta sealed the letter, then did her best to hurry to the door. She swung it open and smiled at the petite young woman on the other side. "Please see Ruth and Abby into the parlor and tell them I will be with them in a moment." She held out the letter to the maid, her expression now all seriousness. "And please make sure this gets into the post today. This is a special letter. Here is the cost of postage." Henrietta dropped several coins in Nancy's hand. The price of smuggled mail had increased in the past weeks. "And this is for your continued discretion," she added dropping a few extra coins in the maid's hand.

"Yes, ma'am. Thank you." Nancy dipped into an elegant curtsy, a wide toothy smile on her face.

"No. Thank you."

Nancy dipped into another curtsy, then dashed off to complete her delivery. Henrietta closed the door behind the maid and set about getting ready. She tucked her feet into her slippers, then looked down at herself. She wore only her wrapper, since stuffing her aching body into layers of fabric, hoops, and corsets held as much appeal as a trip to the surgeon.

It was nearly half-past eleven, and under normal circumstances, she wouldn't be dressed so informally this late in the day. But it was only Ruth and Abby. They wouldn't have any qualms with her receiving them dressed so casually. Deeming her current state of dress acceptable, Henrietta left her room to go meet her friends.

The sight that greeted her when she stepped into the parlor left Henrietta momentarily speechless. She stared at her friends, mouth ajar, debating if she'd somehow stepped through a rip in time and space and entered someone else's home. Ruth and Abby were in front of the bay windows, with Ruth staring daggers at Abby, who paced at a fast clip. They argued about something Henrietta was too shocked to pay attention to.

"Ruth! What on earth happened to your hair?" Henrietta asked, her brain still trying to process what she saw.

Ruth's hair was... gone.

"Thank you!" Abby threw her hands up as if praising the heavens for someone else who saw reason. "I asked the same thing, and the fool had the nerve to tell me it was nothing."

"Because it is nothing." Ruth ran a hand over the small crop of tight curls that still remained of her previously thick, mid-back-length hair. There was only an inch or so left. She pulled her bonnet lower down her forehead, hiding her shaved scalp.

Henrietta stepped up to her friend, her brow furrowed in concern. Running her hands up and down Ruth's arms, she tried to make her voice even and nonjudgmental. "What's going on, Ruth? You know you can tell us anything."

Ruth twisted her gloved fingers, unable to meet Henrietta's eyes. Finally, she squared her shoulders and lifted her head. "I'm enlisting. I'm going to be a soldier."

Henrietta knew whatever Ruth was going to say would be bad, but this was downright terrifying. Enlisting? Had she and Thomas been drinking from the same contaminated cup of water? What on earth was she thinking?

"As in you plan to be a soldier in the army? That's absolutely nonsensical," Abby said, stealing the words from Henrietta's mouth.

Henrietta vigorously nodded in agreement. "Agreed."

"Listen." Ruth walked to a chair and dropped into it with a determined huff. "I've already made up my mind, so there is nothing either of you can do to stop me. At this point, all you can do it support me or leave me to it. Although, I hope you will support me, since there is no one else I can share this decision with. And if I am being honest, it scares the dickens out of me."

"Oh, Ruth." Henrietta rushed to her friend's side and wrapped her in a tight hug.

Close on her heels, Abby sat on the other side of Ruth and did the same.

"We love you so much," Henrietta said. "Both of you are like sisters to me. I could never see you come to harm. That would kill me."

"Agreed," Abby seconded.

Ruth laid her head on Henrietta's shoulder and folded her hands in her lap. "I know. And I hate to do this to you, but I must. I've been thinking long and hard about how I can make good on our pledge. I don't have special skills like the both of you."

"Yes, you..." Abby started.

"And that's all right. What I do know is that I can ride better than any man, I'm a decent shot, and I can occasionally follow orders." They all giggled at the thought of Ruth taking orders from anyone. "After what happened on Monday, my eyes have been opened to how much this war needs to end. The Union must win if we're ever going to have a chance at transforming into a society where all men are seen as men. This is our homeland too, and I want to help make it one in which we can all thrive."

Henrietta and Abby stared at each other over Ruth's head. Her sad eyes and deep frown told Henrietta Abby didn't like this plan any more than she did. But what could they do?

Ruth had made up her mind and would be a soldier, whether they liked it or not. At least they could send her off knowing they would be waiting when she safely returned home. And give her the confidence to know that she would.

Donning an encouraging demeanor, Henrietta squeezed Ruth's shoulder and patted her twiddling fingers. "Well, if the haircut doesn't convince them you're a man, the foul vocabulary you like to use certainly will."

Ruth's lips curled into a mischievous grin. "Can't argue you with you on that point."

Abby giggled, causing a chain reaction of mirth, until they were all sprawled across each other on the couch, laughing uncontrollably. These would be the moments Henrietta missed the most during their time apart. Prayerfully, the war will be won sooner rather than later, and the time wouldn't be long.

"Ruth is going to be a soldier. Henrietta is part of the Black Militia for Union Victory. I need to hop to it and make good on my pledge." Abby pulled away from their group hug and scratched her temple as if in deep thought.

"Actually," Henrietta said in a sheepish tone. "My uncle visited yesterday and revoked my admission into the militia. He said he couldn't see me in harm's way or something along that vein."

"Oh no, sorry to hear that," Abby said.

"Don't fret. I'm working on a plan that will force him to let me in."

"Do tell," Ruth said, leaning over and giving Henrietta her full attention.

Henrietta held her hands up. " I'm sorry, ladies, I can't go into full details at the moment. I must take certain precautions to protect the identity of the other person involved in my plan."

"Ooh," Abby cooed. "Secret plans. Mystery accomplices. I do love a good intrigue. Once the war is over, you must tell us everything."

"If it is safe to do so, I promise I will."

"Good. Now on to the last item of business," Ruth said, her demeanor taking on an air of seriousness. "Your mother made mention that Elijah saved you from your attackers. Spill. We need every single detail. Don't even think about leaving anything out." She placed her elbows on her knees and cradled her chin in her hands, a knowing gleam sparkling in her eyes.

Abby's entire being lit up as if she'd just been told heaven was real, and her entry was guaranteed. She clapped her hands so fast that they were no more than a flapping blur.

"Yes! Tell us everything. It must have been dreadfully romantic. Well, not the being attacked part. That must have been terrifying. But did your heart race and butterflies swarm in your stomach when he came to your rescue? Was he all manly and heroic when he fought those ruffians off of you?" She cocked her head to the side as if struck by a new thought. "Did he fight them off of you? Did..."

"All right, all right," Ruth cut in, waving a hand in Abby's face to shush her. "Let the woman answer some of the questions before you fire off more. We'll be dead and buried by the time you finish asking. I want to know what happened, so hush up."

Abby folded her arms and trained her scowl on Ruth, her mouth pressed into a thin line. After a momentary staring contest, they both turned to Henrietta, their expressions expectant. Henrietta's shoulders slumped a tad as she retreated into herself. The events of her assault were what they were, and she couldn't blame her mother for sharing them. But how she wished she hadn't.

Henrietta's entire face flamed. Neither Ruth nor Abby would care that she'd fallen asleep in Elijah's arms that night. Lulled by the smooth baritone of his voice as he told her stories of fairies and ancient kingdoms. Or that she'd fought her sleep as long as possible to steal a few more minutes with him. But still, the thought of divulging those things made her feel exposed and vulnerable in a way she wasn't ready for.

She cleared her throat, delaying her confession for a few more seconds. "Yes, Elijah saved me. And yes, being cradled in his arms while he carried me to the carriage was the safest that I've felt in a very long time. I'd give anything to feel that way again. But that will never happen."

She purposely left out his late-night visit and her subsequent offer of taking him on a picnic. Those were things she wasn't ready to tell anyone, including her best friends.

Abby's face scrunched in disappointment. "And why not?"

"Because the color of my skin is not the same as his, and in our world, that can be the difference between life or death. The rioting is a testament to that. It wouldn't be proper to flirt with temptation, knowing nothing can come out of it. Besides, I'm meant to marry Matthew."

"Horse shit." Ruth smacked her thighs and vehemently shook her head. "I'm not saying you should harbor notions of marrying Elijah, but why can't you enjoy his company? At least for now. Live for yourself, just this once." The corner of her mouth curled into a devious smile. "You can taste Elijah's forbidden fruit, then settle into an unfulfilled life with Matthew later."

She couldn't do that. Could she? Henrietta bit the inside of her cheek and drummed her fingers on her knee.

"Very rarely do I agree with Ruth," Abby said. Her forehead wrinkled, and she tapped a finger on her chin. "And I don't agree with *everything* she's said on this subject, either. But I do believe you shouldn't close yourself off to what could happen between you and Elijah. I think you should explore it and see where life takes the two of you. It won't be easy, but nothing in life worth having comes without a struggle."

"That's true, but..."

"No buts. Stop *thinking* about it and *feel* it. Does it feel right? I think the two of you were made for each other, honestly."

Ruth snorted. "I won't go as far as our overly romantic friend and say you belong together, but I can see the attraction between you two. He looks at you as if he wants to devour you, cuddle with you, and spank your bottom all at the same time," she said, waggling her eyebrows suggestively.

"Ruth!" Henrietta dipped her chin to hide the red-hot flush she knew even her russet-brown skin couldn't hide. Leave it to Ruth to make her feel completely embarrassed yet emboldened to let her thoughts run wild with salacious images of Elijah's large, calloused hand on her round bottom.

"What? I've known you for years, Henrietta Catherine Wright. I know all your tells, and each time you look at Elijah, I swear you're going to rip off your dress and offer yourself up to him to do as he pleases. You can't pretend to be a prude around me."

Well, there's a visual.

Henrietta fanned herself as new images bombarded her mind. Her beneath Elijah in his bed. His lips traveling over her body. His hands buried in her curls, massaging her scalp. Good thing she hadn't bathed as of yet. Thanks to Ruth, once they left, she'd now need to take a very cold bath.

"My goodness, this conversation has taken a rather lustful turn. Shall we start a new topic?" Abby said, fidgeting in her seat.

For someone who griped fairly regularly about having no color to her skin, Abby's face was brighter than a perfectly ripe strawberry. Henrietta didn't know whether to laugh at her crimson friend or chastise the other for having such a foul—albeit truthful—mouth.

"A new topic sounds lovely." Henrietta sat up straight, a metal pole replacing her spine, and folded her hands in her lap. "The weather outside is rather lovely today, is it not?"

"Lovely indeed," Abby replied, before giggling.

"Fine. I'll allow the topic change. But one day, I really do hope you get out of your own way and let yourself taste the kind of bliss that can only exist between a man and woman who actually enjoy each other's company. Especially if you plan to resign yourself to being a board beneath Matthew for the rest of your life."

Henrietta cringed at the thought of sharing a marriage bed with Matthew. His touches and kisses had been getting harder and harder to endure as of late. She'd treated him so poorly when he'd come to visit. Maybe there was a scrap of wisdom in what Ruth was telling her. She needed to get Elijah out of her system. To touch the flame of passion that smoldered between them. Perhaps if she did, the allure of forbidden desire would wear off, then she could focus on her real future.

But how would she do it? And what exactly would this exploration entail?

Slow down. You don't have to know everything from the beginning.

Henrietta closed her eyes and took a deep breath to calm her ragged nerves. Take it one step at a time. That was all she had to do. And her first step would be taking him on a picnic. Easy enough. She hoped.

Chapter Eleven

One horse stall cleaned. Two more to go. Elijah wiped his forearm over his face. He was covered in sweat, grim, and a layer of horse matter he didn't want to think about. If he hadn't gone nose blind to the smell already, he'd probably gag on his own stench.

He'd been working harder than usual today. His need for a distraction from his thoughts— more specifically, thoughts of a particular brown-skinned beauty—had increased tenfold since the other night. Henrietta was so far above his station; he'd make better use of his energy trying to capture a star than fantasizing about ever having a future with her.

Unfortunately, his heart didn't seem to care what his brain had to say on the matter. It harbored visions of Henrietta curled in his lap, her head resting against his chest, while his hands ran through her soft curls. It remembered how they'd talked for hours, and longed for another such conversation. About what, he didn't know and didn't care. As long as she was there with him, he'd be content.

"Elijah? Are you in there?"

Henrietta? What was she doing in the stables? Had she come looking for him? The hairs on Elijah's arms rose to attention as if they wished to wave and let her know, yes indeed, he was here.

"Yes. Last stall."

Her footsteps echoed through the wooden building, coming closer. His heart galloped in his chest like an untamed mustang. His hands grew moist around his pitchfork as he waited for her to enter the stall. He smelled Henrietta seconds before he saw her. Cinnamon and woman.

She stepped into the stall, a shy smile playing on her luscious full lips. How many times over the years had he imagined kissing her until she opened up to him both physically and emotionally? It would be too difficult a task to try and count.

"Ah. There you are." She tucked a few stray curls hanging at her temple behind her ear. Her eyes flicked to the ground, then back to his. "I hope you don't mind my intrusion, but I..." She clasped her hands in front of her, then quickly released them, balling them into fists at her sides. "I wanted to ask if you would like to go on that picnic I invited you on."

She made her declaration with so much resolve, Elijah sucked in his lips to keep from laughing. It was as if she'd been warring within herself about whether or not to extend the invitation and then concluded that doing so was what she truly wanted and would not cower from the task.

Elijah looked down at his dirt-covered clothing. "I'm sorry, *a stór*, but I fear I'm in no condition to go off on a picnic right now."

"Oh, I didn't mean... It doesn't have to be right this second. Whenever you're ready. Today. Tomorrow. My schedule has some flexibility in it. I'm..." Her chin dipped and her arms curled around her middle. Her cheeks quickly lifted then fell in a stiff smile. "I'm going to be quiet now. I think I've blathered on long enough and you understand my meaning."

Elijah couldn't contain his laughter any longer. This was a completely new side of Henrietta. Flustered and stumbling over her words on his behalf. He'd be a liar if he said it didn't make his chest swell, and elation fill him to the point that he wanted to howl like an alpha wolf.

He reached out to touch her but remembered the dirt on his hand, so he let it fall to his side. "I have another idea."

Henrietta looked back up at him, her curiosity apparently dimming her embarrassment. "An alternative to the picnic?"

"Yes. Coming dancing with me."

"Dancing?" she shuffled her feet, kicking at the hay.

Elijah leaned on his pitchfork, trying to give off an air of confidence he didn't actually feel. As if her rejection wouldn't cut him down. "Yes. Dancing. I know the perfect place. We'll have a great time."

Henrietta nibbled her bottom lip. "When?"

"Tonight."

"Tonight?"

Despite the fear of her rejection crouching beneath his composure, it was quite entertaining to watch the usually eloquent Henrietta Wright turn into a parrot.

"Yes, tonight. We can leave after dark, so no one will know we're gone. It's only a half-hour ride. And we can stay for as long or short a time as you wish."

"Where is this place, exactly?"

"That's a surprise. Do you trust me to take you there and return you home unharmed?"

Henrietta closed the distance between them, then gripped his wrist and forearm with both her hands. She nodded her head, her expression all seriousness. "Yes. Yes, I trust you with my life. I'm sorry if I made you question that. I'd be thrilled to go dancing with you."

This woman! Elijah didn't blink. *Couldn't* blink for several seconds. He didn't want to miss even a second of drinking in her angelic face. She was concerned he doubted her trust in him. He'd meant nothing by his question, but she'd taken it to heart, going so far as to declare she trusted him with her life.

He wanted to scoop her in his arms and kiss and worship her until she felt in her very soul how much he cherished those words. His heart leapt into his throat, wanting to be closer to the glorious woman who made it feel like it could grow wings and fly.

Elijah wiped his hand on his pants, then reached out and stroked her cheek with his thumb. He needed to touch her so badly. To be connected to her in some way. He nearly crowed when instead of pulling away, she pressed her cheek into his hand.

"I'm sorry. You didn't make me question your trust. I was making a rather poor attempt at a joke. But thank you for your assurance. If you don't wish to accompany me, please don't feel obligated to say yes."

"I want to. I think we'll have a marvelous time."

Elijah withdrew his hand and took a step back. He needed space to gather himself and refrain from doing anything that would ruin the moment. Like taking her in his arms and kissing her until she begged for more of his touch, his passion, even his body over hers. Or more likely, slapped him across the face and called him a wretched deviant for forcing himself upon her.

He cleared his throat to rid his voice of the gruffness of desire. "Meet me back here after sunset."

"I will."

Henrietta took several steps backward, then finally turned and exited the stall. He watched the sway of her hips as she walked, pretending they had an extra sway in them just for him.

When she was out of sight, he tightened his grip on the pitchfork and went back to work. He moved with even more fervor than before. The sooner he finished, the sooner he could get back to his room and start the process of making himself look presentable. He glanced down at himself. He'd need all the time he could get because it was going to be a long process.

Elijah checked, then rechecked his appearance in the oval full-length standing mirror crammed into the corner of his room. Everything remained in order, yet he couldn't pull his eyes away from his reflection. Something was amiss. It always was. But this time, he would find it before he went to meet Henrietta.

He gripped the side of the mirror and leaned in, using his mental list to assess his appearance one last time. Face scrubbed clean. *Yes.* Dirt removed from beneath his fingernails. *Yes.* Shirt pressed and wrinkle-free. *Yes.*

Not a single thing was out of order, and yet, his worries wouldn't leave him be. He gave his cheek a heavy-handed smack to wake himself up from his unrelenting foolishness. A nice cherry whelp in the shape of his hand formed on his tan skin. He cursed himself under his breath. If there had been nothing for Henrietta to point out before, now he'd created it out of his own stupidity.

He pinned himself with a hard stare. "What are you doing?" he paused as if his mirrored self would answer. "Worrying over your appearance like some lovesick pup."

Even after that rather rousing speech, his eyes never strayed from his reflection in the glass surface. Why couldn't he rid himself of the need to look perfect for Henrietta?

Because you love her, you lout.

What man didn't want to present his best self for the woman he wanted to impress? But as true as that might be, he needed to relinquish his compulsion to look perfect and finish getting ready.

His room was a complete mess. Shirts and trousers littered his bed, strewn across it in his frenzy to find a suitable set of clothes. Or more so, to find something that would make him look half as presentable as the pompous arse Matthew. His limited wardrobe of four good shirts and two pairs of trousers didn't leave him much to work with.

Henrietta agreed to go dancing with you, not that flapdoodle.

He smiled at that thought. It was true. She said yes to him, knowing what he did and didn't have. He didn't have to be anything other than himself.

With renewed confidence, he looked himself over once more. "This is as good as you'll get, and that's good enough."

He grunted at his reflection and rubbed a hand over his freshly trimmed beard, then turned his back on the mirror. Too much more looking at himself and he'd be late. He snatched up his jacket and headed out the door, stuffing his hands through his sleeves as he went.

Hands clapped. Feet stomped. And cheerful voices carried over the fast-paced melody set by the fiddlers filling the barn with music. People danced about, kicking out their heels, then stepping in a line to the left then right.

Everyone was having such a good time. Colored and white people danced together as if the ugliness of the war waging outside hadn't penetrated this little haven. Henrietta moved closer to Elijah. It made no sense, but a tendril of anxiety snacked through her, twisting and churning her stomach.

There were so many people. So many faces she didn't recognize. Her breathing quickened, and the moisture evaporated from her mouth, leaving her tongue a dehydrated log stuck to the roof of her mouth.

Elijah bent down to whisper in her ear. "You're shaking. What's wrong?"

"I... I don't know. I think I'm... scared."

Scared. Standing in the middle of a barn filled with happy, dancing people she was scared. Terrified, really. Henrietta folded her arms around her stomach, tears stinging the back of her eyes. They'd done this to her. The men who had attacked her. They'd created this irrational fear and stolen her ability to enjoy an evening spent dancing, surrounded by new people who could have been new friends. For the first time since the assault, seeds of bitterness took root in her heart.

Elijah laced his fingers through Henrietta's and gave her hand a gentle squeeze. "Look at me, *a stór.*"

Warmth, comfort, and a sense of security flowed between them. Henrietta slowly lifted her eyes to his.

"I will never let anything happen to you. I would fight angels and demons to keep you safe. No man will ever make it through me to harm you. Do you believe that?"

Henrietta pressed closer to Elijah's side. She squeezed his hand, a peaceful smile on her lips. "More than I've ever believed anything else."

"Then, shall we join in? I by no means claim to be an expert dancer, but I can move to the beat."

Elijah shuffled his feet in time with the music, then bent low in an exaggerated bow, his hand extended to Henrietta. She giggled at his antics, her fear and apprehension fading away. He'd saved her from her assailants. He chased away her doubts. He made her smile. Elijah truly was an extraordinary man in so many ways. And she felt blessed to share in this small portion of his life, even if their time together wouldn't last forever.

The shadow of sadness tried to creep into her mood, but before it could take over, Henrietta accepted his offered hand and pulled Elijah to the edge of the throng of dancers. They jumped right in, hooking their arms and spinning in a circle, then switching partners again and again, until they came back together once more.

Henrietta never took her eyes off of Elijah, no matter who she danced with. He was her anchor. Her safe harbor in the tumultuous storm of doubt and anxiety lurking at the edge of her consciousness, ready to strike and destroy this good time. She and Elijah moved in time with the pulse of the music and the steps of the other dancers.

The night wore on, filled with nonstop revelry. Henrietta whooped and laughed until her cheeks burned from so much smiling. She couldn't stop watching Elijah laugh and joke with everyone. He was so relaxed and carefree. This was a side to him that she'd yearned to have access to for so long. Even when her feet started hurting, and her legs grew tired, she pushed herself to keep going. This night was the best she'd had in a long time, and she never wanted it to end.

Chapter Twelve

Henrietta hiked her skirt around her ankles and spun in a clumsy circle, humming the tune of the song that had played during her and Elijah's last dance. She tilted her head back, basking in the feel of the cool breeze on her warm skin. What a marvelous night. They'd danced, laughed, met wonderful new people, and had an all-around good time.

Tonight might well have been the most fun she'd had in ages. Henrietta sashayed along the dirt path leading to the hitching post where their horses were tied, playing the evening over in her mind. There was nothing about it that she would change.

The clomp of the horse's hooves against the hard dirt grew louder, signaling that their journey home was upon them, dampening her mood.

"Must we leave?" Eyes downcast, lips pouting, she added a hearty amount of sulking to her voice. "One last dance. Please. Why can't we dance one last time?"

Elijah playfully nudged her with his shoulder and offered her a bemused smile. "That's what you said after the last four dances. For someone who was reluctant to be here at first, you've become fond of late-night barn dances rather quickly."

"That's because I needed this more than I realized, and I don't want the good time to end." She twirled in a circle around Elijah, batting her lashes at him in a feeble attempt to distract him from insisting they return home.

He chuckled and shook his head at her, not slowing his swift steps. "The answer is still no. We need to leave. I have to get you home before night's end. Your mother will mount my head on the wall if she finds out I took you here without a chaperone."

"And what a handsome wall mount you'd make," she said, tilting her head and biting her bottom lip in a flirtatious manner.

Henrietta's cheeks warmed. Where had that declaration come from? What wanton woman had taken hold of her tongue? Elijah suddenly halted, nearly making her run into him. His steady gaze found and held hers. Henrietta lowered her lashes, proving the bold woman of seconds ago to be a fraud.

"You think me handsome?"

Henrietta went so still; she wasn't sure if she remembered how to breathe. Could she—should she—answer him truthfully? She licked her lips to delay her reply and moisten her now parched skin. She looked up. Passion, hope, and uncertainty, all reflected back at her from his stormy blue eyes, giving her the strength to speak.

"The first time you walked into my classroom, my world tilted on its axes. Your very presence sucked me into a new world of longing and hasn't let me go since."

A low growl deep in his throat was the only warning Elijah gave before grabbing her by the waist and pulling her flush against him. His hungry lips swooped down, cutting off her gasp and devouring her mouth. Henrietta threw her arms around his neck, holding on with all her strength for fear of letting go and destroying the enchantment of the moment. He sucked, nibbled, and kissed her lips, taking and giving pleasure like nothing she'd ever experienced before.

This couldn't end. She needed this night to last until the day she breathed her last. Elijah's hands dug into her hair, massaging her scalp and holding her in place for his ravaging kiss. His deft fingers made quick work of her ribbons and hairpins, freeing her thick curls, which tumbled over her shoulders and down her back.

Henrietta pressed herself into Elijah, wanting every part of her body to touch his. Good. His lips on hers felt so good. More. She needed more. His arms banded around her, squeezing tight until she could hardly breathe. Still, she didn't pull away. One minute her feet were on the ground. The next, she was lifted off her feet, floating through the air until her back connected with something rough, grooved, and hard.

Pinned between a tree and Elijah's strong body, Henrietta used all of her senses to memorize every part of him. She touched, tasted, and inhaled the glorious, rugged man who ignited a desire in her she'd never dared hope to attain. She savored the thrill of the new sensations awakening inside herself.

"Stop," Elijah breathed, breaking the kiss and shattering the haze of desire surrounding them.

"We have to stop. I'm sorry. I shouldn't have done that. I shouldn't have kissed you."

He placed her back on her feet and pulled away so quickly that Henrietta swayed, almost falling forward without him there to keep her steady.

She pressed her fingers to her swollen lips, too shocked to do anything other than blink. "What? You're sorry?"

"Yes. I'm sorry for losing control like that. I shouldn't have touched you so inappropriately. We should leave."

Sorry? Mistake? After a kiss filled with that much passion, he couldn't really mean that. Henrietta searched his face for any sign of his true feelings but found nothing in his closed-off expression. The sultry carnal desire of seconds ago no longer burned in his eyes. He shoved his hands in his pockets, his eyebrows pinched together, and turned away from her. Did he truly think what they'd just shared was a mistake? She didn't. Far from it.

"Yes. Mistake," Henrietta said, her voice little more than a dejected whisper. "It was a mistake."

She folded her arms around herself, eyes cast to the ground, longing for the sky to open and hurl a lightning bolt to put her out of her misery. How embarrassing. She'd poured every ounce of yearning she'd felt for him over the years into that kiss, and he thought it as nothing more than a mistake. Something he wished never happened.

Silly girl. Wanting things you were never meant to have.

Henrietta trailed silently behind Elijah. For women from her social sphere, destiny wasn't something chosen but assigned. She would marry a well-bred man and give birth to his babies. She'd clean and run his house, never expecting so much as a thank you. If she were lucky, the marriage bed wouldn't be a complete burden or at least something she didn't have to endure often.

"No!" Henrietta said in a soft voice. She stopped walking and concentrated on what she'd just said. "No," she repeated, louder this time.

Elijah turned around, his eyebrows scrunched together, and scratched his head. "No?"

"Yes. No!" Henrietta lifted her chin in defiance.

"I don't understand what you're trying to say."

"No, it wasn't a mistake. Far from it. That kiss was one of the best experiences I've ever had, and I won't let you cheapen it by denying the power I know you felt, same as me."

Elijah said nothing for a long time. He stood there, staring at her through the darkness. "I'm the son of an Irish immigrant who couldn't be bothered to take care of his son past the age of twelve." He held out his hands. "I've shoveled manure, scrubbed floors, and worked fields with these hands. They are calloused and rough from years of hard labor. And they couldn't point to the proper utensil to use during each course of a fancy dinner party. These hands aren't worthy of touching and holding a woman like you."

"'A woman like me?' What does that mean?"

"An educated woman of means from a good family. You deserve so much more than I will ever be able to give you, Henrietta. I can't sully you by tasting what was never meant for me."

"What was meant for you?" Henrietta placed her small hands in his much larger ones. She captured his gaze, refusing to let him look away. "What do you think was meant for the man who comes to my aid when everyone else turns away? The man who risks his own safety for mine. The man who takes me somewhere he thinks I will enjoy, instead of a boring social gathering for the sake of appearances. The man who wants me for no other reason than I am who I am. Why can't a woman like me be meant for a man like you?"

"Those things will not put food on the table or keep a roof over your head."

"But they can fill my heart and soul with a joy most people never experience in this life." Henrietta cupped the side of his face. "I can't make you any promises. I don't know what can come of this, but I would like to..." She paused and thought for a moment. "Well, I guess I don't know what I'd like to do exactly."

The color of their skin, the beliefs of many of their fellow countrymen, and the laws of their country hadn't changed. All those things stood in opposition to their union, so what could they really hope for?

Elijah captured her hands again and kissed each of her knuckles. "How about for now we simply enjoy each other's company? No promises. No pressure."

"Yes. Let's do that." Henrietta smiled up at him, her triumphant giddiness spilling forth.

"If we're truly going to explore a friendship, then we need to be alive to do it." Elijah gently squeezed her fingers. "Come on. Let's get you home before your mother finds out. Else she'll kill us both."

"All right, all right. Let's be off then."

Elijah laced his fingers through Henrietta's and led the way to the horses. She glanced at him, making sure he paid her no attention, then touched her lips, cheering to herself. He'd kissed her! He'd finally kissed her, and it was even better than she'd imagined. A new warmth crept up her neck and spread over her cheeks. Ruth and Abby were going to tease her for days, if not weeks. That kiss was worth the impending ribbing. All she could think was, when can we do it again?

What on earth had she done? That question had been playing on an endless loop since Henrietta had awakened. In the light of a new, euphoria-free day, the decision to refute Elijah's claim that their kiss had been a mistake shone for the horrible blunder it was. How could she fix this without hurting his feelings?

Shoulders slumped, head hanging, and gaze fixed on her feet, Henrietta drug herself up the last few steps, then shuffled to her room. She had a lesson plan in need of review for tomorrow evening's class, but she couldn't take hold of her worrisome thoughts long enough to concentrate on the task. Enjoy each other's company. As if they could. She'd been born with the manacle of certain privileges around her neck, and with that came specific obligations.

Being a colored woman born free. and to a family with means, was a liberty not to be taken for granted or treated carelessly. She couldn't squander a privilege so many wished they'd had. Her mother had drilled into Henrietta for as long as she could remember that she owed it to her people to marry a colored man of means, so they could contribute to the betterment of their society. And she'd agreed. So why couldn't her unruly heart get on board with that plan?

Henrietta pushed open her door, then stopped cold. She looked over her shoulder and scanned the hall to confirm no one else was around to see the incriminating result of last night. Clear of anyone else around, she slammed her door shut and rushed to her desk. Right in the middle of the wooden surface lay a purple tulip on top of a letter with her name written in bold, masculine print.

She stroked a finger over the beautiful petals. A heady smile pulled at the corners of her mouth, but she pressed her lips together to keep it at bay. Elijah knew her favorite flower. When had he taken the time to learn it? What else did he know about her?

Not that knowing the answer to those questions changed anything. She couldn't allow her feelings for him to deepen. Friendship. Amicability. Platonic affection. That's all that could exist between them. Yet she couldn't banish the itch in her fingers to snatch up the letter and tear it open to see what he'd written her. Giving in to the urge, Henrietta plucked the note off her desk and opened it.

"Meet me in the stables at quarter past four."

That's it? She flipped the letter over. Nothing. No explanation of why he wanted her to meet him or what they would do. She pulled out her pocket watch and checked the time. She had an hour. Plenty of time to convince herself that meeting Elijah was a bad idea and she shouldn't do it. Or that it could be the continuation of something dangerous and irresistibly delicious.

Chapter Thirteen

Henrietta peered from the parlor, around the corner, and scanned the hallway. It was empty. At the very end was her target. The door leading to the fastest route to the stables. Now all she had to do was sneak down the hall past the kitchen and dining room without anyone noticing. Easy enough.

Not hearing any noise from either of the rooms, she tiptoed forward, pausing every few seconds to glance over her shoulder and confirm she was still the only one about. *Almost there.* A few more steps and she'd be out the door and well on her way to another secret rendezvous with Elijah. Something that would be wiser to avoid. She reached for the handle, a thin sheen of sweat covering her hand.

"Ah, there you are darling," her mother said from behind her. "Going somewhere?"

Henrietta went still, an icy lump of dread knocking her heart from her chest to her feet. She searched her brain for a reasonable half-truth about what she was doing. Nothing came to her. The worst thing about fear was its tendency to block the ability to think clearly at a time when it was needed the most. Henrietta turned slowly in an attempt to by herself more time before answering. Her mother stood at the bottom of the stairs, patiently waiting for her daughter's reply.

Face schooled to what she hoped portrayed calm composure, Henrietta forced a smile. "Good evening, Mother. Yes. I was going to go for a quick ride before sunset. I'm in need of a little fresh air."

Her mother's lips pressed together in a grimace. She folded her hands against her stomach, a sign Henrietta had come to recognize as concern for her only child. "Are you sure you're feeling up to it? There is nothing wrong with lying about for a while."

"I've never been one to lay about, and you know it," Henrietta said, her apprehension easing and her smile becoming a little less forced.

"True. Very well. Be careful and don't do anything too strenuous. I think I saw Elijah head to the stables not too long ago. Have him ready a horse for you."

"I will."

"And before I forget, we need to invite Matthew and his mother over sometime soon. Your courtship has gone on for quite some time, and I think it's time decisions were made. I want to have grandbabies before I'm too old to play with them."

Her mother's pointed stare narrowed ever so slightly. Odds were Henrietta was imagining it, but there appeared to be a hint of suspicion and knowing in her mother's expression. She couldn't possibly know what Henrietta had been up to last night. Before she'd left, Henrietta had checked to make sure her mother was sleeping. The small blessing of living with a woman who rose with the sun was that she went to bed well before it set.

Henrietta brushed off her absurd wariness and nodded. "Yes, Mother."

She hustled out the door before her mother could say anything else. Or before the volcano of reasons she didn't want to marry Matthew erupted, spilling words she wouldn't be able to take back.

Elijah felt Henrietta before he saw her. His heart tripped over itself, then picked up its pace from a slow jog to full sprint. Henrietta entered the stables wearing a plain, pale yellow dress that made her skin glow. He'd always loved that color on her.

"Hello, Elijah," she said in a small voice.

"Hello." He'd spent the majority of the morning worrying she wouldn't show up. From the way she alternated between running her hands down her dress and clenching, then unclenching, her hands, he'd been right to worry.

"So, what's the plan for today? I assume it has something to do with riding."

"Your assumption is correct. We're going on an adventure, which is why you'll need these."

Elijah pulled a stack of folded clothes from behind his back and held them out to Henrietta. Her gaze bounced from his face to the clothes, then back to his face. Taking the stack, she unfolded the first item, shook it out then held it up between them. Elijah watched her eyes grow almost comically large.

"Breeches? Why are you giving me men's clothing?"

"As I said, you'll need them for our adventure. You can change in that stall there if you like. I'll step outside."

Henrietta didn't move. She continued to stand there, holding out the articles of clothing and staring at them as if she were trying to solve a math problem that contained no numbers. Blast it all. He'd overstepped. In his mind, the plan had sounded mysterious and romantic. Now he could hear the perverseness of handing a woman a pile of clothing then telling her to change into them in a smelly horse stable. Nothing about this was going as smoothly as Elijah had hoped.

"Or..."

"No, it's all right. But I'll um... I'll need help with the ties on my dress."

She turned and lifted her hair, moving it over her shoulder, exposing the laces on the back of her bodice. Now it was his turn to falter. Elijah rubbed the back of his neck with one hand and shoved the other in his pocket. Help her undress. How much self-control did she think he possessed?

Henrietta glanced over her shoulder; her eyes filled with patient expectation. She trusted him.

Both to take her on this trip without telling her the destination, and to help her undress without mauling her like a crazed lust-filled beast.

He could do this.

For her, he would do this.

Elijah took a step forward. The delicate feminine fragrance tinged with cinnamon that was all Henrietta assailed him. He closed his eyes and took a long deep breath. His nostrils flared as he tried to inhale enough of her scent to imprint the smell on his memory.

Opening his eyes, he reached out a shaky hand toward the laces of her dress. He paused inches away and let his hand hoover there. The thunderous boom of his heartbeat in his ears made it nearly impossible for him to think straight.

Make quick work of it, then shove your hands back in your pockets.

Elijah exhaled a steadying breath, then swiftly unlaced Henrietta's dress.

He'd almost made it through the entire ordeal as a complete gentleman, when Henrietta's sleeve slid down her shoulder, pulling down her chemise and exposing the barest trace of her smooth tawny brown skin. Elijah traced the line of her shoulder, hypnotized by the softness beneath his finger. Perfection. Everything about her was exquisite.

Giving in to every fantasy he'd imagined over the last two years, he bent and kissed the crook of her neck.

Her breath hitched. The hiss of her sensual exhale drove him wild and ignited the firestorm of desire that only burned for her. He straightened, back rigid, and stuffed his hands in his pockets. "I'll wait for you outside."

Elijah jogged out of the stable. He feared moving any slower than a run would lead him to give in to the temptation the scoundrel inside him wanted, but the gentleman inside him resisted. Being an honorable man was going to be the death of him.

Steady streams of warm sunlight swept down Henrietta's back as she rode through the open field to a destination Elijah had yet to share with her. White billowing clouds drifted across the clear sapphire sky, looking so soft and fluffy she wanted to reach up and pluck one from the heavens.

Elijah couldn't have picked a better day for a long ride through the countryside. Too bad the sun had already begun to set. If they didn't make it to their destination soon, they'd be forced to come back another day. Unless his surprise was something they could do in the dark. *Oh no*. A swarm of images of her and Elijah in compromising positions surrounded by darkness flooded her. Why couldn't she banish such base thoughts?

Henrietta's cheeks warmed. For the umpteenth time since the incident in the stable, she wondered if this outing was a good idea. Phantom tingles of his lips on her shoulder kept her shifting her position in the saddle to ward off the sensual desires he'd stirred in her. She held no illusions about having control over her attraction to Elijah. Hence her riding next to him now when she should have kept her distance. Under the right circumstances, who knew what could happen between them.

"May I now know where we're going?" Henrietta asked, needing something to focus on other than the low hum of passion between them.

Elijah grinned at her. "Patience, a stór. Our destination is not much further."

"We've been riding for over an hour. We left the borders of the city a long time ago. There probably isn't another soul around for miles." Henrietta swept her arm out, emphasizing the emptiness of the sprawling meadow.

"Good point. Luckily for you, that means there will be no one to see you lose this race. Yah!" Elijah dug his heels into the horse's side, sending it flying at full speed.

Henrietta's grip loosened on the reigns. She was momentarily too shocked to move. A slow smile built on her lips as the surprise wore off. "Oh no, you don't. Yah!"

She squeezed her thighs against the horse's sides, sending it galloping after Elijah. She leaned low and close to the horse's neck, enabling them to move faster. The distance between her and Elijah quickly vanished. Snapping the reigns, she pushed the horse harder until they passed Elijah.

"You go ahead of me. You don't know where we're going," Elijah said in an amused tone.

Henrietta glanced at him over her shoulder but didn't slow her horse's pace. "Doesn't matter. As long as I beat you, I'm headed in the right direction."

"The first one to the tree on the top of that ridge wins."

Henrietta zeroed in on the tree in question. That was all she needed. A final destination to mark the place where she'd claim her victory. It couldn't have been more than eight hundred yards away, at the top of a small hill. Her mother always chastised her about not letting her competitive nature get in the way of behaving with class and dignity, but right now, she didn't care. Racing with Elijah, being driven by adrenaline and exhilaration, made her feel alive and free. Henrietta tugged on the reigns and leaned to the right, then left, then back to the right. Following her commands, the horse zig-zagged in front of Elijah, blocking him from passing her.

"I'd call you a cheat," he shouted over the pounding hoofbeats, "but you'd probably call me a sore loser."

"You'd be right," Henrietta called back.

She smiled so wide she was sure all her teeth were on full display, even the chipped incisor on the bottom. The rhythm of her heart matched the barreling tempo of the horse's hooves pounding on the dirt. Elijah's smooth rumbling laugh fanned the jovialness spurring her onward. The tree grew taller the closer she got until it was a mighty looming entity stretching high into the sky.

"Come on, girl, just a little farther," Henrietta whispered into the horse's ear as both an apology and command for the horse to move faster.

The gap between her and Elijah widened, but not for long. His horse gained on hers but never surpassed them, making her wonder if he was letting her win. No matter, she'd claim the victory and refrain from pointing out her suspicion.

"I did it. I won," Henrietta crowed when she reached the tree.

Her horse pranced in a circle, then settled in place and munched on the tall grass. Adrenaline pumped through Henrietta, making it hard to fight the urge to send her horse galloping off again. But the poor animal needed to rest. She'd ridden the old girl hard.

"Now, where are we going?" she asked when Elijah came up beside her.

"Right here." He leapt from his saddle, then ambled to the side of Henrietta's horse and helped her down. "Follow me."

Henrietta stood rooted to the spot, unable to believe what her eyes were seeing. Elijah walked up to the tree, then grabbed a thick branch, planted his foot against the trunk, and climbed up. Did he really bring her all the way out here to climb a tree? Apparently, he had. He straddled a sturdy branch, then leaned back down, his hand outstretched to her.

"Come on. We don't have all day."

Elijah stared at her, patient expectation shining in his eyes as if he had no doubt she would do as he said. He was truly insane. And she must have lost her marbles as well because she traipsed over to the tree and took his offered hand, shaking her head the entire time. Her mother would have a fit grand enough to make the devil run and hide if she saw Henrietta with one arm wrapped around a tree branch and the other around Elijah as he hoisted her up. He kept climbing farther up and repeating the process of stopping to help her up until they were a good distance from the ground.

"If you drop me and I break my neck, I will haunt you for the rest of your life," Henrietta warned, between ragged, huffing breaths.

"Not much of a threat. I'd enjoy that very much."

"You're right. Maybe I should..." Henrietta's foot slipped, her frightened gasp swallowing the rest of her sentence.

Elijah's iron grip tightened on her hand. His other arm shot out, wrapping around her back to keeping her from falling. With one big heave, he hauled her the rest of the way up next to him on the branch.

"I got ya. No need to worry." He held her tight as if trying to prove she'd always be secure in his arms. The tiny circles he rubbed all over her back soothed her frayed nerves.

Henrietta rested her cheek against his warm chest, taking the comfort he gave. "Thank you."

Yet again, he saved her. Plucked her from the clutches of imminent danger. He was her gallant knight and rescuer. Henrietta's heart flip-flopped back and forth inside her chest. How was she supposed to convince herself to stay away from him when he kept doing things like that? Not that she was doing a good job of it anyway. Henrietta sighed, wanting to protest when his hand stopped moving.

He tapped her shoulder, then pointed at something behind her. "Look, a stór. This is what I brought you here to see."

Careful not to move too quickly for fear of tumbling to her death, Henrietta scooted on her bottom, rotating in the direction he indicated. Her breath caught at the magnificent sight that greeted her.

Streaks of burnt orange stretched across the sky, colliding with cranberry and violet clouds. The colors bleed down to the earth, creating an ethereal ambiance over the landscape. Divine. Exquisite. Mesmerizing. It was all those things and so much more. The best painter in the world could never fully capture the grandeur of the scenery laid out before her. This was a masterpiece only the Almighty himself could craft. Birds floated through the air with slow grace, wanting to enjoy the beautiful sunset as much as Henrietta.

"It's stunning," she said with reverence.

"I stumbled upon this place years ago after my dad left. While sitting up here watching the sunset back then, all I could do was wonder, 'where did the sky end?' It spread from here all the way back over my old home in Ireland. Out to California, where my dad said he was heading. I figured I couldn't be the only person under that beautiful sunset wishing their life was different. How many people sat under a similar sky, hoping for something bigger, something more? It made me feel not so alone."

Henrietta shifted positions; her entire attention riveted on Elijah. "I'm so sorry. How old were you?"

"Twelve. My old man said I was old enough to start fending for myself. Well, that's what the letter he left me said."

Twelve? What kind of father abandoned their son on the streets of New York at such a young age?

If her memory served, Henrietta recalled Elijah once telling her that he came to America shortly after this tenth birthday. His father left him alone in a harsh city, in a country he hardly knew. Her heart broke for the sad, lonely, little boy he must have been.

"Well, it's his loss. He missed seeing you grow into the wonderful man you are today."

Elijah shrugged off the compliment, averting his gaze. He didn't let her go, but Henrietta had the sneaking suspicion it was only because they sat so high up in the tree. If they were on solid ground and he didn't need to protect her, he'd pull away from her both emotionally and physically.

"He's not missing much. Not like I made anything out of my life. I'm a former pickpocket, turned dock worker, turned domestic servant. Not much of a life worth celebrating."

Henrietta flinched. Not because she felt any ill will from him about his position in her household. But because of all the dreams he must have that she'd never cared enough to ask him about. She'd spent so much time trying to keep her distance and avoid any romantic temptations between them, she'd forgotten to simply be his friend. To see him as another human with ambitions and dreams for their life.

"Tell me something," Henrietta said, touching his cheek to guide his attention back to her. "If you could do anything, be anything, what would it be? What are your hopes and dreams?"

Elijah pressed his face into her hand, then kissed her palm. "I've always wanted to be a doctor," he answered without hesitation. "I want to study the art of curing human ailments others."

A proud smile pulled on the corners of Henrietta's lips. A doctor. She could envision him helping and healing people of all races and backgrounds. He'd probably make no money, though. Instead of charging for his services, he'd take whatever his patients could offer, be it chickens, vegetables, or nothing at all. Henrietta chuckled to herself. Either way, he'd be a well-respected and trusted man in his community.

"That's a very noble profession. I think you'd make an excellent doctor."

"Thank you for your confidence in my potential."

Henrietta could almost hear the "but" in Elijah's tone. He appreciated that she thought he'd make a great doctor, *but* it would never happen.

Elijah pressed on Henrietta's shoulders, spinning her back around to look at the sunset, ending this line of conversation. She wouldn't badger him about it. At least not right now.

She could understand his doubt about obtaining such a future. In spite of her family's wealth, in the eyes of some, there would always be a cloud of otherness and inferiority hanging over her head because of the color of her skin. The society they lived in was built on the principle of elevating some by crushing others. He was the abandoned son of an immigrant who, until the last several years, hadn't been able to read or write. Few in his situation fooled with the notion of hoping for more from life.

But so help her, Henrietta was determined to help him do exactly that.

"Thank you for bringing me here. This is truly magical."

"Thank you for coming with me."

Henrietta settled against his chest. Elijah probably didn't catch the double meaning of her last statement, but she'd show him how much this time together meant to her soon enough. A new plan began forming in the back of her mind. She tucked the idea in a special place in her heart for safekeeping.

Chapter Fourteen

There is nothing I would not do for those who are really my friends. I have no notion of loving people by halves, it is not my nature.

The truth of those words leapt off the page as Henrietta reread the lines from *Northanger Abbey* for the third time. Miss Austen had captured her current mood perfectly in those two sentences. She didn't know how to love halfway. For her, it was all or nothing.

Which was why she should have stayed away from Elijah. And why not doing so had resulted in her current predicament. Daydreaming about an evening spent wrapped in his arms, watching an exquisite sunset, not wanting to be anywhere else, or with anyone else. And going over all the reasons she shouldn't have gotten him a special gift she hoped he loved. And she couldn't dismiss how much she missed simply being near him, even though she'd seen him this morning and spoken to him every day for the week that followed their outing.

The scariest part about it all was that the reasons for staying away from him in the first place were becoming less and less important with each passing hour. Societal pressures, her mother's expectations— everything else didn't matter in comparison to the joy she'd found with Elijah.

Henrietta reviewed the new spelling list one last time, humming an upbeat tune and fighting to keep a smile off her face. "Stop it right now," she chastised herself. She knit her eyebrows together and purposely frowned in an attempt to dampen her jovialness. "You have things to do, such as finishing this lesson plan. He's only a man. You're not in love with him."

At least she wouldn't admit it if she was. Henrietta scribbled her last few notes on the paper in front of her, then checked her pocket watch.

"Oh, goodness. I'm late."

She'd spent so much time daydreaming she hadn't kept a careful watch on the time. Snatching up the papers, she dashed around her room, grabbing her bonnet and shawl. She was down the stairs and pulling the front door open in record timing. Unfortunately, the person standing on the other side halted her departure, stealing the minutes she'd recaptured.

"Matthew?" she said more as a question than a greeting. "Um, hello. What are you doing here?"

He bent and kissed her cheek. "Hello, my dearest sunflower. I came to escort you to your class. I feel as though we haven't been able to spend much time together as of late."

"Oh. I..." She scrambled for something cute or affectionate to say, but nothing came to her. Well, nothing that applied to him. "Thank you," she said lamely.

His arm jutted out, extending a bouquet of roses to her.

Roses. A flower that, although beautiful, was not her favorite. Something a man she'd been courting for nearly three years should know. But why would he? Her favorite flower was one of the many things Matthew did not concern himself with learning about her.

Unlike Elijah.

Every time she spoke, Elijah's attention was riveted to her every word. He'd once stared so intensely at her lips while she talked, she'd thought he was trying to memorize the shape of them. *Ugh. Stop it!* Since when had her brain taken it upon itself to keep track of the vast differences between the two men?

She accepted the offered token of his affection, cradling it in the crook of her arm. As if conjured by her greatest dream or worst nightmare, Elijah chose this time to round the corner of the house. His long stride faltered when he looked at her. Hurt, accusation, and anger flashed across his expressive face before he shrouded his emotions behind a stony wall of indifference.

Henrietta wanted to hurl the flowers to the ground as if they'd suddenly become a cluster of venomous vipers. Her cheeks warmed, and she cast her gaze to the ground, unable to withstand the guilt looking at him incited within her. Several days ago, he'd kept her safe in his arms as they sat perched high in a tree watching a breathtaking sunset. Every day since they'd stolen opportunities to talk, flirt, and be in each other's company.

Now here she was, accepting flowers from another man.

"Shall we be off then?" Matthew asked, oblivious to the emotional war raging inside Henrietta. The self-absorbed man probably hadn't even noticed Elijah pass by.

"Yes. Let's," Henrietta said, needing to be away from the weighty guilt threatening to drown her beneath its brutal waves.

Per the appropriate protocol, she latched onto Matthew's arm when he extended it to her. He took a few steps, then stopped when she didn't move. Henrietta blinked several times, then looked down at her feet, shocked they weren't moving.

"Did you forget something in the house?" Matthew asked.

It was a logical conclusion for him to come to, for why else would she have not moved after consenting to walk with Matthew to the place she'd just been rushing off to?

"No. I thought I did, then remembered I packed everything," Henrietta lied.

"Very well, then."

Henrietta gave Matthew a weak smile. What was the matter with her? She needed to hurry up and compose herself.

You don't want to go anywhere with this man, that's what's the matter.

Brushing off her truthful, yet unhelpful thoughts, Henrietta recovered, then fell in step beside Matthew. They headed off on the brisk journey to the schoolhouse in amicable silence.

"It is such a lovely day, is it not?" Matthew asked.

Henrietta held in her groan. She'd rather walk in quietness than engage in meaningless conversation. No, that wasn't true. If she were walking with Elijah, she'd talk about the weather, dead languages, even the details of watching grass grow. She'd talk about anything, as long as she was speaking with him.

"Very lovely indeed," she replied, forcing herself to engage in small talk. "What are your plans for the rest of the day?"

"Mr. Brown will be coming by the shop for his final fitting this evening." Matthew puffed out his chest, his nose lifting in the air, and grabbed the lapel of his frock coat with his free hand. "He's a banker, and I'm making him a brand-new wardrobe of suits. He heard about my unrivaled tailoring skills from a colleague and after our first meeting, decided that I'd be his personal tailor from then on. I don't blame him. I am the best in the city if not the state. Maybe even the entire country." He chuckled to himself as if he'd just told the world's most amusing jest. "I will make him the envy of every gentleman he meets. No doubt he will be sending so many new clients to me, I'll have to turn some away."

Such superficial arrogance, it was almost nauseating to behold. Henrietta's lips pressed into a thin line. She prayed the full extent of her uninterested cynicism wasn't written clear as day across her face. Did he really think bragging about himself and tossing the status of his clients in her face was impressive? The smug grin on his face said he did. Yet another example of how little he knew about her. She didn't care one iota about such things.

"Very impressive," she said in a tight voice. "You know, I was thinking..."

"Oh, one second, darling. I wasn't finished yet. I'll let you speak in a moment."

Henrietta bristled. The hairs on the back of her neck stood on end. *Let me speak?* What kind of authority did this arrogant, pompous ass think he held over her? More than he actually did, which was none. The nerve of some men.

"As I was saying..."

Matthew's meaningless prattle fell on deaf ears. Henrietta stared ahead of them, nose wrinkled, and brows drawn together in disgust. *Elijah would never...* The remaining words of that thought pelted her stomach like the icy bullets of a winter soldier. Elijah this. Elijah that.

It was time for her to face the truth.

She had feelings for the man.

Feelings she shouldn't have. Shouldn't act upon. But they were there, nonetheless. If she were truly honest, she'd have to admit they'd been there for a very long time. The butterflies have certainly existed since the first time he walked into her classroom.

Henrietta suddenly stopped moving, forcing Matthew to halt next to her.

"Why are we stop..."

"I have to end our courtship," Henrietta blurted out.

Matthew's head snapped back as if she'd slapped him. His arm fell to his side as he took a step back. "I beg your pardon?" he said, looking at Henrietta as if she'd suddenly transformed into a misshapen creature he didn't recognize.

"I have to..."

"Yes. Yes. I know what you said, but what do you mean?"

What did he mean, what did she mean? The words seemed pretty clear to Henrietta. She squinted at him; her head tilted ever so slightly. How was she supposed to answer him? Her words could not get much plainer than the ones she already used.

Matthew closed his eyes and pinched the bridge of his nose, his face lifted toward the sky as if sending up a silent prayer. Eyes popping back open, he shook his head and speared her with a disappointed scowl as if she were a naughty child in need of a reprimand.

"You can't end our courtship. I've waited nearly three years for you to become my wife. Patience is not a virtue I possess, but I waited because your mother all but guaranteed that you'd be mine. She even promised a sizable dowry after our marriage as a consolation for how long you've made me wait. My family is banking on that money, and by God, I expect you to honor our bargain. I will not leave empty-handed, do you hear me?"

By the end of his tirade, Matthew's light honey face had turned a nasty shade of deep scarlet. His nostrils flared, and his rigid, pointed finger had made its way into Henrietta's face. The wolf had finally shed his sheep's clothing.

"Goodbye, Matthew," Henrietta said in a deadpan voice, her face a cold wall of stoic indifference. She continued on down the road, leaving him standing alone in a cloud of his own righteous indignation.

His words stung, but she'd never let him see how much. She'd had no illusions of a happily ever after with Matthew. She didn't love him, and he didn't love her. But she'd hoped they could at least find common ground based upon mutual respect in their marriage. Clearly, that would not have been the case. She was a prized mare he'd hoped to ride into the land of wealth and status.

Well, he could take that journey on his own, because she'd had enough of him and all the strings attached to being his wife.

"You can't walk away from me," he shouted after her, drawing several pairs of eyes from passersby around them.

"And yet I am," she snapped, not looking back, not stopping, and certainly not apologizing.

Henrietta rolled from her left side to her right, squirming in bed until she found a comfortable position. She tucked her hands under her head and stared unseeing at her bedroom wall. *Why can't I sleep?* She'd been tossing and turning since she went to bed several hours ago. Or maybe it hadn't been hours. Maybe it only *felt* like hours because torturous misery had a way of distorting a person's perceptions of reality.

The hurt and betrayal in Elijah's eyes had haunted her all throughout her lesson, the walk home from the schoolhouse, and the agonizing hours she had to wait until it was an appropriate hour to retire to her room.

But she hadn't betrayed him, necessarily. He'd known her courtship with Matthew hadn't officially ended despite the time they'd been spending together. And she hadn't invited Matthew over. Really, it was all a combination of poor timing and misunderstanding.

So then why did she feel like she'd rolled in a putrid vat of slimy unfaithfulness?

That's it! Henrietta bolted upright and tossed the covers back. Enough was enough. She'd done nothing wrong, and she was going to tell Elijah as much. Never mind the late hour. She was going to march right up to his door and knock until he opened it so she could give him a piece of her mind. She shoved her feet into her slippers and tossed on her wrapper over her nightgown, then made her way to the door, but stopped when something outside her window caught her attention.

Pulling back the curtain a tad, she saw Elijah lying on a blanket out in the garden. *Excellent.*

She could speak to him without fear of anyone else in the house hearing. Letting the curtain fall back into place, she marched out of her room, ready to relieve herself of this undeserved guilt.

Cinnamon and her. Elijah lay on his blanket, hands tucked behind his head, eyes closed, enjoying the cool night air while he waited for Henrietta to approach. Her small feet moved noiselessly over the grass, but he knew everything about her. Including her smell. And even if he didn't, his body could sense her presence like a moth drawn to a flame.

"Hello, *a stór*," he said when she neared.

"Don't 'hello' me. Do you have any idea how you made me feel today? I didn't..."

Elijah's eyes flew open, and he shot up off the blanket, shocking Henrietta into silence. He stalked toward her, hands clenching and unclenching at his sides. Passion and rage churned inside him, causing a volatile storm of unnamed emotions.

"Do I know how I made you feel?" he all but spat. "Do you know you made me feel?"

Henrietta took a step back, then another. "I..."

"Today, I had to watch *my woman* accept flowers from another man. Then she walked off with him, arm in arm, snuggled to his side. It took everything inside of me not to snap that self-important ratbag's neck. I was furious, jealous, and scared because..." he deflated, his shoulders slumping and took a step back. "Because at that moment, I realized how perfect you were for each other. He is everything I'm not. He has everything I will never have. Money, class, even the right skin tone. I can't give you what he can. What you deserve. And it would be selfish of me to hold you back from those things."

Elijah sunk back on the blanket and pulled his legs up to lock his arms around his knees. Henrietta stood over him, saying nothing. He couldn't bring himself to look at her. It would be too painful to stare into her eyes when she told him she agreed. That he wasn't good enough for her.

"I..." she stammered. "I ended my relationship with Matthew," she said in a voice so soft he wondered if he heard correctly.

His head snapped up, and their gazes locked. Her eyes glistened with uncertainty and hopefulness. Could he have heard what he thought he did? "What did you say?"

Henrietta dropped to her knees beside him and threw her arms around his neck. "It's over.

My courtship with Matthew. I won't marry him. I *can't* marry him.."

When Henrietta pressed her soft, full lips to his, a colorful array of fireworks exploded in Elijah's heart. The kiss was tender and sweet at first. Her lips pecked over his, hesitating every so often, exposing her inexperience. Not that he'd had many lovers either. Working long hours doing back-breaking labor didn't leave one with much time to purse pleasures of the flesh.

After his initial shock wore off, Elijah wrapped his arms around Henrietta's waist, pulling her closer until she straddled his lap. He deepened the kiss, sliding his tongue over her lips until she opened for him. Sweet. Savory. Delicious. She tasted like his wildest dreams come to life. His hands sprawled across her back, exploring and pressing her further into him.

Never breaking the kiss, Elijah spun them so that Henrietta lay beneath him on the blanket. Her low moan flowed into his mouth, through his entire body, setting his blood on fire. *More*. He needed more. There would never be a day when he'd had enough of kissing her. His lips traveled across her cheek, behind her ear, and down her neck. He bunched the fabric of her

skirt in his fist, ready to tear away the barrier
keeping his hands from touching her skin.

"Elijah."

She said his name like a breathy plea for
more. Only it had the opposite effect. Elijah
released Henrietta and rolled away to a safe
distance like an unsuspecting cat doused by a
bucket of ice water.

A rosy flush crept over her neck and spread
over her face. Runaway curls sprouted in every
direction from her long, unraveling braid. Her
parted, kiss-swollen lips gulped down air into
her starving lungs, which expanded her chest,
offering up her round bosom to his hungry gaze
with every breath she took. Her wide eyes stared
up at the night sky, a litany of emotions running
through the desirous haze covering them.

"Why..." She touched a hand to her lips then
turned to look at him. "Why did you stop?"

Passionate fire surged through Elijah anew.
Disappointed. Henrietta was disappointed that
he'd done the gentlemanly thing and let her go.
Too many more questions like that, and he
might not be able to restrain himself again.

He chuckled, the corner of his mouth lifting
in a wicked grin. "You left me no choice. Your
kisses are the sweetest poison that makes me
forget how to act with honor. A second more

and we would have been naked in the grass putting on a show for everyone in the house to witness."

Henrietta flipped on her stomach and scanned the windows of her home. They all remained dark and showed no signs of anyone moving about. Even in the moonlit darkness, Elijah could see her blush had deepened from rosy to scarlet. He fought back a full, hearty laugh at the worried expression on her face.

She sat up, tucked her legs beneath her, and hugged her arms around her middle, then speared him with a serious gaze. "I meant what I said. I can't marry Matthew. I don't love him and as much as I thought I could withstand a loveless marriage, I can't because... Never mind." She tucked a stray curl behind her ear. "I'm still not making any promises about us or what can come of our relationship. But I'd like to explore it. That is if you'd like to do the same."

Elijah closed the distance between them and gently caressed the side of her face. "I'd love nothing more." He gave her a quick, chaste kiss on the lips, then released her.

She smiled at him. A candid, joyful smile that stole Elijah's breath.

"Good." She nodded once. "We'll have to be more discrete in the future."

"We'll be so discrete, people will think we've become ghosts." He winked, earning another charming smile and husky laugh.

Henrietta scooted close to him and gave him a quick peck on the cheek, then stood. "Good night, Elijah."

"Good night, *a stór*."

"I've been meaning to ask you about that name. What does it mean? Is it Gaelic?"

"Yes, it is, and I will tell you one day when the time is right."

"You'll have to teach me someday. Not just that word, but everything. Your language, history, customs. I want to know it all."

Elijah swelled with pride for his homeland. He felt larger than life itself, hearing Henrietta's desire to know more about the land he loved so much and would forever consider home. She wanted to know him. All of him.

"Yes. One day I shall. Good night."

"Night."

He watched until she was safely back in the house, then laid back on his blanket and stared up at the starry night sky.

Perfect. She is absolutely perfect. And she's mine. My a stór.

Chapter Fifteen

"All right, Mr. Jolly, last one and then I must be on my way," Henrietta said to Mr. Johnson, standing next to her at the front of the classroom.

Two years later, and the old man still came up to her at the end of every lesson with a new set of jokes. She had to admit each one made her laugh as much, if not more so, than the last. Today, she was especially grateful to him for giving her an excuse as to why she couldn't help smiling and was brimming with merriment. Better to blame it on the sweet older gentleman with the infectious laughter than the real reason.

"You sure? I could let you go now if you got someplace to be."

"No, it's fine. Please continue. I'm rather fond of today's round of jokes." She gave him an encouraging nod.

Mr. Johnson tucked his thumbs in the suspenders of his pants, then rocked from the balls to the heels of his feet. "Okay then. Stop me if you heard this one. A preacher walked into a brothel and said..."

"Good afternoon, Mr. Johnson," Abby called, stepping into the nearly empty schoolroom. "Hello, Retta. I have the book you requested."

"Well hello, Miss Sunshine," Mr. Johnson replied, a warm twinkle in his eyes.

Abby ambled up to the pair, oblivious to her interruption. "You're looking more dashing than usual Mr. Johnson. Is that a new hat?"

Mr. Johnson preened like a peacock showcasing its feathers. He tilted the straw boater hat toward Abby. "Why, indeed it is. Got it last week."

"I like it a lot. Makes you look sophisticated and cultured."

Mr. Johnson spread his feet wide and placed his fisted hands on his hips. If he lifted his head any higher, he'd be able to smell an incoming thunderstorm. Henrietta covered her mouth to keep the giggle tickling the back of her throat from spilling out. Flattery or not, Abby never failed at making Mr. Johnson feel as important as a king, and Henrietta loved her for it.

"Thank you kindly. Well, I will let you ladies be. The missus has been complaining about me running my mouth too much after class and not making it home before sundown to help her finish the gardening. Pleasure seeing you as always, Miss Sunshine. And can't wait until the next lesson, Miss Retta."

"Same to you," Abby replied.

"Don't forget we'll have a quiz," Henrietta said.

"I won't. Y'all take care now." Full of happiness and smiles, Mr. Johnson waved goodbye, then left the room.

Abby turned her attention to Henrietta and held out the book she'd been cradling against her chest. "*The Principles and Practice of Modern Surgery* by Robert Druitt, per your request."

"Thank you!"

Henrietta took the heavy book and opened it to a random location. Sketches of human body parts and proper treatment methods for various injuries filled the pages. It was perfect.

"Care to tell me what you need it for?"

"It's a gift for Elijah."

Abby's eyebrows shot into her hairline, and her eyes stretched so wide, it was a wonder they didn't pop out of their sockets. "Details! I need details."

" Let's see..." Henrietta tapped a finger on her chin, pretending to think about what had been transpiring between her and Elijah. As if she hadn't been consumed with such thoughts every second of the day. "Ah, yes! He took me dancing and to see the most beautiful sunset." She peeked around the room and lowered her voice even though there was no one else there. "And we kissed."

"You what? Oh, my goodness. You didn't! You did!" Abby squealed and danced in place. Calming just a little, she grabbed hold of Henrietta's hands and squeezed. "Was it the most romantic thing you've ever done? Did you like it?"

"Yes," Henrietta mumbled, a warm flush heating her cheeks. "And I loved it."

"I knew it! I knew he was the one for you. I am so happy for you."

"Let's not get carried away. I said we kissed not ran away and eloped."

"Not yet." Abby gave her a conspiratorial wink. Almost like an afterthought, she asked, "And what about Matthew? What did you do about him?"

"I called off my... whatever it was with Matthew. I don't love him. I thought I could endure a marriage with someone I have no feelings for, but now every time I think about sharing a bed with him, I feel like a million tiny ants are crawling under my skin."

"What a visual." Abby laughed so hard that Henrietta couldn't help but do the same. "Well, what about Elijah? Does the thought of sharing his bed make you think of ants?"

"More like butterflies. Millions of them, fluttering around in my stomach until I find myself pressing my hands against my belly to keep them contained."

"I knew it. I called it. Ruth owes me a dollar!"

"You two were betting on the status of my romantic life?"

"Of course we were. It's the most exciting and uncertain thing any of us have done in ages."

They both laughed even harder. Henrietta couldn't deny the truth in that statement. Trying to figure out the right path to take in her love life was a rather daunting and equally exhilarating undertaking. She still didn't have a final answer.

Abby sobered. She clasped her hands behind her back and nudged the ground with her big toe. Her classic habit for when she had bad news to share. "Speaking of Ruth, I'll be leaving in a few weeks. I'll be going with Jonathan to tend the wounded on the battlefield. I believe we will be somewhere in Virginia. I don't know when we will return."

Henrietta nodded in understanding. What she really wanted to do was list all the reasons Abby needed to stay put right here. The main one being her safety. The thought of losing Abby too tore her heart out. But they'd all made a promise they were determined to uphold.

Besides, who was she to lecture anyone on engaging in risky activities? Henrietta awaited a letter, against the law to send in the first place, from her contact so she could convince her uncle to let her join the Militia.

"I will miss you greatly, but I know our time apart won't be long." Henrietta took Abby's hands in hers. "Looks like everyone is making good on their vow except me."

"You'll convince your uncle to let you join the Black Militia, and even if you don't, it might be for the best. What Ruth and I are doing is dangerous. If your uncle keeps you out of this maddening war, at least one of us will be guaranteed to survive it."

Henrietta fixed Abby with a stern gaze, squeezing her hands to emphasize her seriousness. "Never say such a thing again. You and Ruth will be fine. Don't you ever doubt that."

"Yes. You're right," Abby said with a small smile.

"I know I am. Now come on, let's get out of here." Henrietta dramatically fanned herself, as if she were on the verge of passing out from heatstroke. "This heat is blistering enough to make me want to strip naked and run through a field to feel a cool breeze on my skin. Since that's not an option, how about we stop and get ice cream?"

Abby's face lit up as if she'd been offered a king's ransom instead of a sweet cold confection. She quivered, her eyes closing, and a dreamy expression coming over her face. "That sounds heavenly at the moment."

"Excellent. Today is feeling like a chocolate kind of day."

"Every day is a chocolate kind of day," Abby said with a giggle.

Henrietta looped her arm through Abby's and lead her out the small schoolhouse. Ruth and Abby would make it back to her. She believed that. She *had* to believe that. Any other outcome was not an option because her world would never be the same without them.

"There you are!" Henrietta nearly skipped down the steps toward Elijah. Her eagerness to give him his gift made it impossible to keep the bubbly smile off her face. He was going to love it, and she couldn't wait to see his reaction.

Elijah unfurled from his crouched position in the flower bed beneath the front porch. The single dimple in his right cheek when he looked at her sent a surge of effervescent gaiety exploding in her chest like the grandest fireworks display ever seen on this side of the grave.

"Good afternoon, *a stór*. You seem particularly happy today. May I ask the reason?"

"This." Henrietta held out the brown paper wrapped item nearly bouncing on her toes as she waited for him to take it.

A minute. Ten seconds. She couldn't hold back from giving Elijah his present for even the briefest moment. She'd planned an elaborate scheme of tempting and intriguing him before handing over the gift, but now her desire to see how deep his dimple caved when he saw what she'd gotten him was too great.

"What is this?" he asked, taking off his dirt-stained gloves, then stuffing them in his trousers back pocket.

Henrietta shook the package in front of him. "Open it and see."

Laughing, Elijah took the present from her, then brought it to his ear and shook it. "Hmm. It's not hollow." He laid it flat in his palms. "It's weighty. Did you get me a brick? I've always wanted one of those."

Henrietta laughed at his absurdity. "Hurry up and open it already."

"All right, all right. Only because I fear if I don't, you'll take my head off."

Elijah tore through the brown paper, crumbling it in his hand instead of tossing it to the ground. He laughed aloud when he uncovered enough to see what it was.

"A book. How very teacherly of you."

Like a snail making its way across a rock on a hot summer day, his laughter dwindled, and his smile slowly faded, then disappeared completely when he finally read the title. Henrietta nibbled her bottom lip. Oh no. Had she made a mistake? Was the gift too personal?

"Is it too much? You said your dreams was to become a doctor. I wanted to encourage you." Henrietta rushed out. "Did I…"

"It's a wonderful gift." Elijah grabbed her hand, interlocking their fingers. "It's thoughtful, inspiring, humbling, and the best gift I've ever been given. Just like you. Thank you."

Elijah bent and kissed her cheek, right there on the front lawn for anyone to see. An action so natural it took a minute for it to dawn on Henrietta to check if someone had noticed. And when it finally did, she didn't care if they had.

This man was everything she needed, and more than she could have known to want.

"Good." Henrietta's smile returned, brighter than before. "I was worried for a moment. I'm glad you like it."

"I love it. Thank you." Elijah kissed her knuckles. "Do you think I can do it? Become a doctor someday?"

"With everything inside me. I have the utmost confidence in you. And whatever I can do to help, I will."

"Thank you. It means the world to me to know you have faith in me. Perhaps I can use it to withstand the days I don't have faith in myself."

Henrietta gave his hand a gentle squeeze. "What are your plans for the rest of the evening? I've been meaning to check up on Thomas and Uncle Paul. Perhaps afterward, I can take you on the picnic I owe you."

"That sounds wonderful, but I have a lot of work to finish up before the end of the day. Maybe tomorrow?"

"Lovely. I was thinking we could…"

"Henrietta Catherine Wright," a familiar high-pitched, feminine voice called from across the lawn. "Well, I'll be."

Henrietta snatched her hand from Elijah's so fast she threw off his balance, making him drop the book. She took a step away from him, her heart pounding an unnaturally quick and erratic beat. Her eyes bounced between the book and the two women strolling toward her and Elijah.

What are you doing? Pick up the book and apologize to him right now.

Despite wanting to listen to her inner voice of wisdom, Henrietta couldn't make herself comply. She stayed frozen in place, the gap between her and Elijah taunting her.

"Silvia. Mary," she said to the women as they strolled up her walkway. "How lovely to see you. What brings you by?"

Unannounced, she wanted to add. Henrietta cringed at the syrupy overly sweet smiles they cast her way. This wasn't going to end well. These two were the worst loose-lipped church gossips.

Not only did they know everything about every colored person on this side of the East River, they had information on a select group of white families as well. Their stockpile of dirty secrets was so high, they could create an avalanche of lies and deception that would wipe out most of Brooklyn's upper-class citizens.

They could only be here for one reason.

"It's good to see you too." Silvia flashed her bright pearly whites in a smile so disingenuous, it put Henrietta in mind of the snake in the Garden of Eden. "We heard about you and Matthew." Her smile instantly transformed into what she probably thought was compassion but looked more like constipation. "We came to offer our sympathies, but it looks like you're doing just fine."

Silvia and Mary pointed gazes shifted to Elijah, who stood blessedly still, his arms crossed, and face neutral. Their greedy eyes swept over his toned, well-muscled body, occasionally stopping to ogle particularly appealing parts of him.

"Yeah. Real fine," Mary chimed in.

Disgust welled inside of Henrietta, making her want to claw their eyes out and spit on them before crushing them beneath her heels.

"I'm surviving but thank you for your concern." Henrietta motioned in Elijah's direction, but couldn't bring herself to look at him. "Ladies, this is Elijah Byrne. He's my... He works for my family."

Henrietta could almost feel Elijah's recoil at her lowly introduction of him. Part of her wished she could take it back, but she couldn't, and that was for the best. These women only needed to know the basics when it came to her relationship with Elijah.

"Ooh, a domestic," Mary all but purred. No doubt, her mind was already weaving a tale about the salacious details of Henrietta's relationship with Elijah. When telling it to others, she'd likely add in plenty of false first-hand accounts of all the inappropriate touches and looks they gave each other in front of her.

Silvia elbowed Mary in the ribs and gave her a withering glare. When she turned back to Henrietta, she'd transformed yet again into the concerned friend and confidant. "If you want to talk about it, we are more than happy to listen. If you need to unburden yourself or anything."

"Again, thank you for your concern, but I don't feel like talking about it at the moment. And if you will excuse me, I have a few things in need of my attention."

"We understand," Silvia said, suspiciously glancing between Henrietta and Elijah.

Henrietta remained stoic, giving nothing of her true feelings away. No doubt, the mere fact that they caught her conversing with Elijah would result in tongues wagging in their social circle for weeks. She might even have to enlist the help of her mother to clean up the ensuing mess that was sure to follow this visit.

She silently cursed herself, them, and everyone else who gave their lies credence.

"You ladies have a good day now."

"You too. Take care." Silvia and Mary strolled down the walkway, huddled together, whispering and occasionally peeking back at Henrietta and Elijah.

When they were finally out of sight, Henrietta released a long, drawn-out sigh. "Well, that was a complete disaster."

"Hmm," he responded with a noncommittal dip of his chin. He pulled the gloves out of his pocket and put them back on. "If you'll excuse me, I have work to finish. Us *domestic servants* don't have much time to waste on idle chatter."

"Elijah," Henrietta said his name like a plea for mercy. "I didn't mean anything by what I said. I'm sorry. Those women are the worst gossips. I didn't want to give them anything to go running their mouths about."

"Yes, like the ridiculousness of exploring a relationship with your penniless servant."

"Elijah, I…" She reached out to touch him, but Elijah stepped out of her reach then turned his back on her.

"Please excuse me," he tossed over his shoulder as he walked away.

Henrietta wanted to call him back. To apologize and beg for his forgiveness. As much as she'd like to lie and say she didn't know her actions would hurt him, she couldn't do so. She'd spurned him to save her own reputation. For that, she would always be ashamed.

Chapter Sixteen

Big expressive brown eyes. Kissable full lips. A quick wit that could put many a man to shame. All the things Elijah loved about Henrietta consumed his thoughts. There were so many reasons that he was never hard-pressed to come up with another.

Those things were why he was going to find her and mend the rift between them. It had hurt the way she'd introduced him to those women, but he could understand. She had to protect her reputation. They'd been living so far in the illusion of a legitimate couple that he'd forgotten what they really were. Nothing.

One thing was certain, he cherished their time together more than his next breath. If all he had were stolen moments until she found a suitable husband, then he wouldn't waste them.

Elijah entered the house and checked the time on the grandfather clock as he passed it. He only had to wait another hour until Henrietta came home. Then he could steal touches, kisses, and moments to drink in her exquisite beauty. He'd made every bargain imaginable with God to be granted his one wish for Henrietta to agree to put the earlier events behind them and carry on as they had been.

"Elijah," Henrietta's mother, Mrs. Wright, called him from the parlor. "Please come here."

He did an about-face and walked back to the room. Standing tall in the doorway, he dipped his head in greeting. "Yes, ma'am. How can I be of service?"

Mrs. Wright sat shoulders back, spine perfectly straight, in a tall wingback chair. Saucer in her left hand and a teacup in her right, she blew on the hot liquid, then slowly took a sip, her piercing gaze never leaving him. Everything about her exuded authority and an acute shrewdness. She slowly placed the teacup on the saucer, then deposited them onto the end table next to her. Folding her hands in her lap, she said nothing. Only stared at him.

Alarm bells trumpeted inside Elijah's head. Something was wrong. She was toying with him. Sizing him up and asserting her dominance. He'd seen such acts performed by men on the streets of the city, right before they beat a man within an inch of his life.

"I received word from Mrs. Andrews, Matthew's mother, that Henrietta has called off their engagement." She quirked an eyebrow at him. "You wouldn't happen to know anything about that, would you?"

The contents of Elijah's stomach rolled like the choppy waves in a brutal storm. An icy fist took hold of his heart, squeezing until the beat slowed to a near stop.

She knew.

Somehow, she knew about him and Henrietta.

He swallowed down his trepidation. "Yes. Henrietta mentioned something about that to me. She said she didn't love him and didn't want to marry him because of it."

"So, you and my daughter discuss matters of her heart, then? How interesting." She picked up the saucer and took another sip of tea, allowing the charged silence to percolate between them.

Elijah said nothing. He stayed perfectly still, waiting for her to make her next move. Mrs.

Wright set the cup down and folded her hands in her lap.

"I recognized my daughter's feelings for you not long after you came into our employ. I regretted the decision to hire you almost immediately. My daughter has a bright future ahead of her. She has the potential to be the wife of an upstanding man in *our* community. As Matthew's wife, she'll be respected and treated as the lady she is."

Elijah didn't miss the emphasis she put on the word "our," but he wanted to make sure he fully understood her meaning. "Do you think I will not respect Henrietta if she were to become my wife?"

"It doesn't matter what you will or won't do. What matters is how everyone else will treat her. You're one man in a very large world, Elijah. You'll love her, but colored people will hate her for betraying her race, and white people will hate her for bewitching you into copulating with a savage heathen. My daughter will have to live in constant fear for her safety, and all the while you'll be inconvenienced at most. You'll escape the truly harmful backlash."

Elijah straightened to his full height. He spread his legs wide and lifted his chin in defiance. "I'd give my last breath to protect

Henrietta from any man. Black, white, or any color in between."

"Marry her, and we might see how true that declaration is," she said in a sharp tone. A beat of silence passed between them, then Mrs. Wright released the weary sigh of a mother constantly battling to protect her child. "Listen, I can see you have real feelings for my daughter. And I know she has them for you. But nothing good can come of it. I know because I've seen it. If you truly care about Henrietta, let her have a chance to live the best possible life. You're poor, Elijah. Nothing to be ashamed of, but a fact, nonetheless. Without money and resources at your disposal to pay people to look the other way, you can't marry a colored woman. Not here. Not now." She stood, her expression imploring. "I'm asking you this as a mother and someone who also loves Henrietta dearly. Will you do this for her?"

She was right. Every single word was an exact description of how Henrietta's life would be with him. Full of struggle and hardship. Rich men did whatever they wanted. Carried on affairs with whomever they wanted. Not poor immigrants.

He didn't have the funds to protect her.

"What would you have me do?" The words left a sour residue on Elijah's tongue.

Mrs. Wright sagged back in the chair, relief washing over her face. She nodded her approval for several seconds before speaking. "You've done wonderful work while you've been here, so I don't wish to fire you. I have an old friend that I'd like you to go see. He lives in Pennsylvania. Stay with him for about a few weeks so Henrietta can spend more time with Matthew. I'll work with him to win her heart. Give her the chance to be happy. Please."

Elijah stuck his hands in his pockets and stared down at his dirty scuffed up boots. "Tulips."

"I beg your pardon?"

"Her favorite flowers. Tulips. Purple tulips."

He looked up, meeting Mrs. Wright's gaze again. Understanding reflected back at him. She knew he was reaching into his own chest and ripping his heart out to place in her hand.

"Thank you," she said in a voice softened by sympathy. "I'll make sure Matthew knows. Now if you could, please go pack your things. I would like you gone before Henrietta comes home."

"Yes, ma'am."

"Thank you, Elijah. I really mean that."

Elijah walked away, unable to force out a farewell. He wanted to howl his frustration and destroy everything in his path. He'd tasted the sweetest of heavens and now had to give it up. The only thing worse than having no hope was experiencing hope, only to have it torn away.

But he loved Henrietta, and part of loving her meant wanting the best for her. He wasn't the best.

"Miss, there's a letter for you."

Henrietta paused at the sound of Nancy's voice, her foot hovering over the first step on the way to her room. It seemed like she'd been waiting an eternity to hear her maid utter those words. She twirled around and hurried over to the other woman. A crinkled, slightly dirty envelope rested in Nancy's outstretched palm. Each crease and streak of dirt on the beige envelope spoke of its journey. How it was smuggled across state lines until it reached Washington, D.C., where the five-cent postage indicated it was mailed from.

"Thank you, Nancy. Your discretion is most appreciated, as always." Henrietta reached into the hidden pocket in her skirt and withdrew the change purse she always had on her in case of emergencies. She pulled out several coins and placed them in Nancy's hand.

The young maid grinned so hard all her teeth were on full display. She handed over the letter and quickly pocketed her reward.

"I will be in my room for the remainder of the day," Henrietta informed her, unable to peel her eyes away from the paper in her hands. "I'm not to be disturbed under any circumstances. Understood?"

"Yes, ma'am."

"Excellent. Thank you again."

"My pleasure to be of service, ma'am." Nancy did a quick curtsy, then shuffled off to handle her other chores.

Henrietta stood in the foyer, momentarily unable to move. This was it. Her key to joining the Black Militia for Union Victory. The bold, masculine handwriting scribbled across the front of the envelope belonged to the one man she trusted above all others. She didn't know exactly what the letter contained, but she knew it would be important and just the right kind of intelligence Uncle Paul couldn't turn away.

She had to open it. The impatient voice inside her head demanded she rip the letter open immediately. But she knew she couldn't listen to it. This could very well be classified information and needed to be treated as such. Reading it in a location where anyone could walk by and see it would be careless.

Henrietta tucked the letter under her arm, then scanned the foyer before dashing off to her room. Adrenaline pumped through her veins, feeding her impatience and spurring her to move faster. She had a coded message to decipher and intelligence to pass along. The excitement of it all was almost too much. Almost.

Oh. My. Goodness. I did it!

Henrietta examined the sheets of paper on her desk one last time. It had taken her the better part of the late afternoon and evening, but she'd finally finished deciphering the letter. She pushed the tray of food Nancy had brought her at supper time to the corner of her desk, creating more space to spread the papers out. Names and ranks of Union soldiers covered the fronts and backs of two sheets of paper. Each man on the list was a prisoner of war being held in a camp near New Brockton, Alabama.

Henrietta didn't know whether to shout in triumph or sob uncontrollably. This was the type of information her uncle couldn't ignore. He'd have to give her a position in the militia once he saw the list. Too bad that honor would be bestowed upon her due to the fact that so many men were being held against their will in what she could only imagine were deplorable conditions. The war had taken its toll on both sides, but it had especially devastated the Confederate States. Food and hygiene products were scarce for soldiers. She could only imagine what supplies for the prisons looked like.

How many of the men on this list had wives and children praying they'd return home someday? And how many never would because of their time spent in that camp?

Hopefully, her small contribution would help ensure their homecoming happened, and sooner rather than later. Henrietta folded the list of names and tucked it into a fresh envelope. She needed to get this to Uncle Paul tonight. After grabbing her bonnet and shawl, she left her room, ready to do exactly that.

Henrietta hurried down the hall but stopped mid-stride after passing the open door of the study. She backed up and entered the room where she should have started her search in the first place. Of course, her mother would be here. The end of the month quickly approached, and her mother insisted on going over the household ledgers herself.

Her mother sat behind the large oak desk in the middle of the room, reading several documents and making notes in her ledger. Even with the combined light of the candles on her desk and those scattered about the room, the lighting was still rather dim. Yet she sat, shoulders back, spine straight, and posture perfect while taking care of her work.

She would have cringed if she'd seen Henrietta hunched over her desk while decoding the letter. The woman believed even the most mundane activities needed to be done with grace and poise. Henrietta supposed one day she'd feel the same. For now, there were more important things to attend to.

Henrietta cleared her throat to gain her mother's attention. "Mother, have you seen Elijah? I wanted him to escort me to Uncle Paul's house."

"It's rather late," her mother replied, not looking up from her papers. "Can whatever it is you need to discuss with Paul not wait until tomorrow?"

Could it? In the grand scheme of things, yes, it probably could. Whether she got the list to him now at half-past eight in the evening or tomorrow would not make much difference to the plights of the men in the camps. However, waiting was not something she could do at the moment. Excited energy coursed through her body, needing her to act right this second.

"It's rather urgent, but it won't take long. We should return within the hour."

Her mother put down her pen and gave Henrietta her full attention. She interlocked her fingers over the pile of papers, her face a blank canvas giving away no hints to her thoughts. That told Henrietta they weren't good, and this conversation was about to turn in an unfavorable direction.

"What's going on between you and Elijah?"

Henrietta's head snapped back as if her mother's words were a physical blow. "I beg your pardon?"

"Answer me. And don't you dare lie."

"I don't know..."

"You have feelings for him."

A statement, not a question. Information her mother had already deemed factual. Nothing Henrietta said next would convince her mother otherwise.

"And if I do?" Henrietta asked in an even tone.

She couldn't let the conversation get away from her by panicking and confessing something she shouldn't.

Her mother slumped back into her chair, for the first time in a long time, no longer concealing her weary exasperation from Henrietta. "You of all people should know that nothing good can come of any feelings you have for him. Why would you even allow yourself to entertain the notion of involving yourself with him?"

"You make me sound like a fool for caring about someone else."

"Yes. For caring about him, a fool is exactly what you are!" Her mother banged her fist against the arm of her chair, silencing all rebuttals from Henrietta. "He is a white man, and you are a colored woman in a country where he has the right to own your very life depending on the location of the dirt beneath your feet. It's hard enough being a woman. Being a colored woman is another layer of struggle in and of itself. Don't add more to your burden than you have to by choosing a man who will toss you to the wolves whenever they start nipping at his toes."

Henrietta took a challenging step forward. She stared down her mother, refusing to relent. "We're not them, Mother! Elijah is not him, and I am not her. I will not base my decision on what is or isn't possible for us based on the past mistakes of others. We will forge our own path and make our own destiny."

"Make your own destiny?" Her mother laughed like that was the most ridiculous thing she'd ever heard. "How? He works for this family. He works for *me*. If ever I decide to let him go, he'll end up back down at the docks, toiling away, never able to scrape together enough to feed and clothe a family."

"You wouldn't dare fire him."

Her mother shot out of her chair, slapping her palms on the desktop and leaning across it. "If you force my hand, I will." She pointed at Henrietta, her dark umber eyes blazing with steely determination. "Matthew is a good man from a well-respected family. You will marry him, and soon. I partially blame myself for allowing you to drag out your courtship for as long as you have. That mistake will be remedied immediately. I'll send word to his mother that in three days, he is to formally propose an offer of marriage, and you will accept."

"And if I refuse?"

"Elijah will be unemployed, and you will be to blame for it. And you will still end up marrying Matthew anyway."

Henrietta and her mother stood there. Staring across the small space between them that might as well have been an entire universe for the little bit of common ground they shared. Henrietta silently cursed her mother for delivering such a harsh ultimatum. Return to how things used to be with Elijah or be the cause of his dismissal. Either way, she would lose him. But at least one of the choices worked in his favor, if not hers.

"As you wish," Henrietta ground out between clenched teeth.

"Good." Her mother sat back down and rested her elbows on the desk, steepling her hands in front of herself. "I will send word to Mrs. Andrews in the morning. And to your original question, I've sent Elijah away for a while, so you can let go of any rebellious ideas you might be concocting."

"What? Where did..."

"That's none of your concern. You may leave now."

Her mother picked up her pen and resumed her analysis of the ledgers. Henrietta watched her mother for a moment, still appalled by the viciousness she'd shown during their conversation. She'd ripped Elijah away from her.

For that, Henrietta didn't know if she could ever forgive her.

Chapter Seventeen

Henrietta sat in her Uncle Paul's study, her leg bouncing and her heel tapping an erratic quick tempo. The cup of tea his maid had poured for her rested in her hands untouched. Elation, misery, hopefulness, and heartache battled each other inside her heart, making her mood as unstable at best, and treacherous in her worst moments.

"Ah, Henrietta," Uncle Paul said, entering the study with long, measured steps. He stopped to place a kiss on her cheek, then continued on to sit in the chair behind his large mahogany desk. "To what do I owe the unexpected joy of seeing my favorite niece?"

"Hello, Uncle. A pleasure to see you today," Henrietta said, ready to be done with pleasantries. She needed action, to get down to business. A distraction from the aches and gnawing pain ripping her heart in two.

"As much as I'd like to believe you, I'd have to say I don't. You look more like a dejected kitten doused with a bucket of water. What's the matter?"

"Mother and I aren't seeing eye to eye on a particular topic, and it is causing a strain on our relationship." Henrietta waved a dismissive hand. "Nothing to be overly concerned about."

Uncle Paul leaned forward, his eyes brimming with empathetic understanding. Henrietta hated it. She didn't want anyone's sympathy. She wanted power. The ability to dictate what happened in her life. To live and love who, and how, she wished.

"Whatever it is, I'm sure the two of you will work it out. Always remember, mothers nearly drive us to the madhouse because they love us so much, they want to protect us from everything. Even our own shadows. Your mother will come around eventually. However, if you're the one being pigheaded, stop it and apologize."

"Thank you, Uncle. I will consider your advice very seriously, as I always do."

"Good." He nodded, satisfied that he'd done his familial duty of giving wise counsel to his young niece in need. "So, what can I do for you today?"

"I want to join the Black Militia for Union Victory."

No pretenses. No verbose speeches meant to persuade. Her patience for such things had vanished. Henrietta stated what she wanted plainly, and matter-of-factly. Ready for the verbal sparring match she knew would follow.

"Henrietta," he said her name like an exasperated sigh. "I've already told you I will not put you in harm's way. My answer remains the same. No."

"Yes, but last time, I wasn't able to prove my value. Last time, I didn't have this." She pulled the folded pieces of paper from her reticule and slid them across her uncle's desk. "After reading that, you won't be able to say no. You'll need me in order to continue receiving such valuable information."

Her uncle plucked the papers from the desk and unfolded them. At first, he read them with the irritated impatience of a father appeasing a petulant child in hopes of making them behave.

His brow pinched, and his frown deepened when the realization hit him of what he read.

"Where did you get this? Who is your source?"

"If I told you, you'd shut me out. I want in." She kept her voice even, despite the exhilaration inflating her ego.

She had him.

Her uncle's grip tightened on the papers, crumpling the edges. "Please, Henrietta. Don't do this to me. Don't make me choose. You're my brother's only child. His daughter. I can't have your blood on my hands."

"You won't." Henrietta sat a little straighter in her chair. She placed the untouched teacup on the edge of his desk, then folded her hands in her lap. "I don't want to do anything particularly dangerous. I only want to help you gather information. That's all."

He cocked an eyebrow, looking at her as if he wondered if she were being obtuse deliberately or if she were so foolish that she couldn't see her own folly. "Do you know how intelligence gathering works in this war?"

Henrietta cleared her throat and fidgeted in her chair, some of her previous confidence deflating. "I have a vague idea, but you can teach me everything I need to learn."

"For the Union, it is an 'every man for himself' arena. The president has his own man to give him information. His man has a man to give him information. There are spies so well hidden you could be sitting next to one, spilling your darkest secrets, and you'd never know they were going to use that same conversation to stab you in the back the next morning. I can't have you talking to the wrong person and getting faulty information or giving secrets to someone on the other side."

"I'm not ignorant of the risks. I accept them without hesitation."

Uncle Paul pounded his fist against the smooth wooden desk. Henrietta jumped but didn't wilt under his forbidding glare.

She wouldn't back down. Couldn't.

"But I don't," he bellowed. "Not where you're concerned. Tell me who your source is, and I will vet them and establish my own line of communication."

"I'm sorry, but I can't do that, uncle. I can't give you my source. You may not trust them, but I do, and they are trusting me. I will not break their confidence."

Henrietta hated the quaver in her voice. Try as she might, she couldn't banish it. But she wouldn't give in to the growling beast her uncle had transformed into. Even if she wasn't determined to join the Black Militia, she loved her contact too much to ever betray his trust.

"Then I'm sorry, I can't accept this information from you." He folded the papers back and held them out to her. "I'll have to treat it as unverified and false. If it is true, think of all these men who will continue to suffer because of your refusal. And you still can't join the militia. That is my final word."

That was unfair. How dare he lay the guilt of the suffering soldiers at her feet? She hadn't started this war. She hadn't captured and imprisoned those men. She was only trying to help.

Henrietta snatched the papers from her uncle's outstretched hand and stuffed them back into her reticule. Rising from her chair, she met his cold scowl with an equally wintery one of her own. If he wouldn't help, she'd find someone who would. Now, more than ever, she had to do this. She needed one thing in her life that she controlled. One thing to banish the helplessness that threatened to consume her.

"Thank you for accepting my visit," Henrietta said in a voice devoid of all emotion. "If you will excuse me, I'll take my leave now. Good day Uncle."

"Henrietta," her uncle said, his voice softening. The menacing glower had vanished from his face.

"Good day."

Henrietta departed without another word. The weight of her uncle's heavy frown followed her as she left.

Air. Henrietta needed a big gulping breath of fresh air. A sea of faces in every shade, from pale as fresh winter snow to dark as a starless night, surrounded her on all sides. Some wore bright smiles; others could barely contain their bored yawns. Henrietta's mood was closer to the latter than the former.

This was her engagement party. A time that was supposed to be filled with almost naïve optimistic hope for the future and love for her partner. Neither of those emotions applied to her. Henrietta wanted to run screaming from the room in search of a safe place, away from the stifling expectations and obligations crushing her under their burdensome girth.

She glanced at Matthew, who stood next to her, chatting with a gentleman she'd been introduced to but couldn't recall his name. They laughed that stiff, disingenuous laugh of men who licked each other's boots in hopes of gaining future favors from one another.

This was her future. Standing silently next to him at parties and gatherings that she didn't want to attend, wishing she were anywhere else. Or with someone else. No, not anyone else — Elijah.

Henrietta took another sip of her champagne, emptying the rest it in one gulp. The effervescent liquid glided over her tongue, tickling her throat on its way down. It was the third — or was it the fourth — glass she'd consumed in the last hour. And the reason the ground swayed beneath her unsteady feet. She scanned the room in search of another butler carrying a tray with more glasses.

From the corner of her eye, Henrietta caught sight of something that nearly made her burst into hysterical tears.

Elijah.

He stood at the edge of the great room, watching her. They stared at each other, not blinking. Three long, torturous weeks had passed since they'd last seen each other. It was terrible for her to admit, but Henrietta was glad to see that looked as miserable as her. Before she was ready, Elijah turned and walked away.

Setting her empty glass on a nearby end table, Henrietta touched Matthew's forearm to steal his attention. "Gentlemen, if you would excuse me. I shall be right back."

"Of course, my sunflower."

Matthew had barely finished his sentence before Henrietta rushed off in search of Elijah. The man without whom, the rhythm of her heart didn't sound the same.

Elijah's heart sank at the patter of Henrietta's slippered feet coming up behind him. He hadn't meant to stop and stare, but she'd been a vision in the golden silk gown that made her skin glow. It had taken all his strength to turn and walk away from her. But by Matthew's side was where she belonged. They made a more fetching couple than he and she ever could.

Henrietta grabbed his arm, moving in front of him and stopping his retreat. Her bright smile was a balm on his fractured soul.

"Elijah? Please wait. Have you just returned from your trip?"

The breathy, hopeful quality of her voice ripped his heart out anew. She was happy to see him. It might not even be a stretch for him to say she was desperate.

"Yes," he answered, unable to meet her eyes. To do so would make him cave to the irresistible temptation of holding her and never letting her go.

"How was it? Where did you go?"

"Good. To help a friend."

Her smile dimmed but didn't vanish completely. Elijah could almost see the spark of determination ignite in her eyes. She wanted a conversation with him, and she'd pull each syllable from between his tightly closed lips if she had to.

"Not very talkative tonight, are you? That's all right. I do believe I've had enough mindless chatter in the past two hours to last for the rest of my life. You wouldn't be in mind of saving me from this gathering, would you?"

Save her. He could almost laugh at the sentiment. He was struggling to keep his head above the roaring swells of despair threatening to pull him under.

"Congratulations," he said, changing the line of conversation.

"Congratulations? For what?" She followed the direction of his finger, pointing at the party. "Ah, yes. My engagement celebration. Thank you."

Silence descended upon them. The awkwardness of it was so painful Elijah almost wanted to engage Henrietta in conversation just to be rid of it.

Instead, he dipped his head and stepped around her. "If you'll excuse me, I need to retire."

"I don't want to marry him," she blurted out, panic welling in her beautiful dark-brown eyes. "I don't love him. I..."

Elijah raked his hands through his hair, releasing a frustrated growl. Why did she have to make this harder than it was? "No."

"No?" Henrietta shook her head, either not comprehending or denying the entire message packed into that one word. "I don't understand."

"You will not harbor foolish notions of having romantic feelings for me any longer. I shouldn't have let you entertain them in the first place."

"Foolish? Let me? How dare you say such things to me?" She glared at him, hands on her hips, and her mouth pressed into a thin line. Blinking away her hurt and indignation, she held up a hand. "Wait. Where is this coming from? Is this because of something my mother said to you?"

"This has nothing to do with your mother."

"It's all right if it does. She spoke to me, as well. I gave in to her demands, which is why I'm here standing next to Matthew when the man I really want to stand next to is you." She gripped his forearm with both her hands. "I shouldn't have yielded. She threatened your job, and I made a rash decision because of it. Please forgive me."

Desperation, yearning, and urgency rolled off of her in brutal waves, threatening to bring Elijah to his knees. Seeing her in so much pain, and knowing he played even the smallest part in her suffering, shattered his heart into a million tiny shards. He covered her hands, taking comfort in their warmth.

"There is nothing to forgive. You made the right decision." Softening his voice, he did what needed to be done and severed the strings tethering them. "Listen, because I will only say this once. Nothing of a romantic nature can or ever will happen between us. What happened between us wasn't real. The thought of you and I together is absurd. I can't save you this time, Henrietta."

Tears spilled down her cheeks. Each one was like a bullet piercing his chest and killing a small portion of his soul.

She wiped angrily at the moisture as if its existence offended her. "I see. If you will excuse me, I have guests to attend to. Good evening, sir."

Elijah balled his fists at his side, his entire body coiled with the discipline needed to hold fast to his resolve and let her walk away. It was for the best. Her mother's speech; the incident with the two women. They'd helped him face a truth he'd been too thickheaded to acknowledge.

Henrietta was a star shining bright in the night sky, and he...

He was the blind man never meant to experience her light.

Chapter Eighteen

Misery loves company.

Now more than ever, Elijah believed in the truth of that saying. He sat in the hallway, his back slumped against Henrietta's door, listening to her anguished sobs. He'd snuck up to her room over an hour ago and hadn't moved since. His muscles ached, and his limbs screamed to be stretched, but he sat motionless, refusing to give his body the relief it desperately desired.

Bastard. Coward. Fool. He called himself all these names and more. Henrietta sat in her room, weeping the most sorrowful cries he'd ever heard all because of him. Because of his carelessness with her heart. Why hadn't he continued to stay away? To let her live her life as she'd originally intended, blissfully unaware of the passion that could exist between them.

Eyes burning from lack of sleep, and holding back his own anguished tears, Elijah internally replayed their conversation at her engagement party. He'd done the right thing, slamming the door on their budding relationship, but that didn't make the consequences any easier to endure.

Henrietta was in pain, and everything in him wanted to burst through her door and comfort her. But he wouldn't. He'd continue to sit here, listening to her suffering, until she'd cried herself to sleep no matter how long it took. A fitting punishment for a scoundrel like him.

A light knock sounded on Henrietta's bedroom door. She stared at the heavy wooden frame with no intention of answering it. For three days, she hadn't moved from beneath the burrow of blankets on her bed for anything other than relieving herself and picking over the trays of food Nancy brought at every mealtime.

Per what had become their unconventional custom, Nancy cracked the door, then stuck her head through, alerting Henrietta to her presence. "Pardon me, Miss. May I come in?"

"Come in," Henrietta croaked through dry lips.

Nancy pushed the door open the rest of the way, entering with the usual tray loaded with eggs, ham, and biscuits. She placed it on Henrietta's desk, then picked up the old one. Henrietta didn't move to retrieve the delicious smelling fare. Her stomach growled in protest of the game of near starvation it had not agreed to be a part of.

"You must think me a fright," Henrietta said with a sad grimace.

Nancy scanned the disheveled mess that had become Henrietta's current state, her eyes overflowing with empathy. "No, ma'am. If I may be so bold, I think you're just a woman experiencing heartbreak. It affects everyone differently, but it hurts like hell all the same."

Henrietta rolled onto her back, staring up at the ceiling, feeling the sting of fresh tears at the back of her eyes. She released an agonized, self-deprecating laugh. "I guess Elijah and I weren't nearly as stealthy as we thought we were."

"Not in the least. We all saw it, probably before the two of you."

"I wish I could have seen how it would end. Then I might not have gone down this path at all."

"Maybe this will lift your spirits." Nancy walked to Henrietta's bedside and placed an envelope next to her on the mattress. "Another *important* letter came for you."

Henrietta lumbered to a sitting position. She stared at the letter, not touching it for a moment. What was the point? Uncle Paul had deemed the information faulty and wouldn't use it. It opened no doors for her. She picked up the letter and opened it. Maybe—as horrible as it sounded—if she deciphered the letter and saw another list of poor men held captive against their will, it would give her a sense of commonality with other suffering souls. At the very least, she'd have something other than her broken heart to focus on.

"Perhaps you're right. Nothing like a little espionage to keep the mind occupied." She tried for a cheery smile. "Thank you, Nancy. I apologize if I don't say that enough."

"You say it plenty but thank you for the sentiment. I'll leave you to it then."

"Thank you."

Henrietta dragged herself out of bed and shuffled over to the mirror on her vanity. She cringed at the haggard, unkempt woman reflected back at her. Wash first, then she'd decode the letter. The time had come and gone for her to pull herself together.

Elijah was only a man. This was her first great heartbreak, but it probably wouldn't be her last. Like many women who'd come before her, she'd survive.

This couldn't be right. She must have misinterpreted something. Because if it were true, then Thomas was detained in a prison camp in Alabama, no doubt suffering unspeakable horrors at the hands of those rebel dogs.

How could that be? Uncle Paul had forbidden him from joining the army. He was only seventeen. Surely, they wouldn't allow him to join without his father's permission. Then again, the army was so desperate for bodies, if he'd lied, no doubt they wouldn't have questioned him.

Henrietta tried her best to set her emotions aside and think back on her last meeting with Uncle Paul. She didn't remember seeing Thomas stalking about the house, but that didn't mean he wasn't there. Perhaps he'd been sulking in his room. *Not likely.* She'd been so wrapped up in what she'd thought was her guaranteed ticket into the Black Militia, she hadn't bothered to ask about him.

Gathering the newest pages filled with the names of captured soldiers, Henrietta prepared to race over to Uncle Paul's house and show him what she'd discovered.

Wait! You can't tell him. Then he'll really demand you give him the name of your contact.

She stopped cold at that thought.

Seeing his son's name on the list would turn Uncle Paul into a desperate father wanting to rescue his son. He'd tear down the entire Confederacy in search of his son. And he wouldn't take kindly to Henrietta's refusal to give up the name of the one person he knew had information on his son's whereabouts.

She couldn't betray her confidant. Besides, what if it weren't Thomas? It could very well be another young man with the same name. She couldn't be sure.

Henrietta marched back to her desk and picked up a clean sheet of paper. She had to go to Alabama and check if it really was Thomas. If it were him, she had no doubt her contact would help her figure out a plan to liberate him from the horrid camp.

She scribbled a quick note to her mother, then set her pen down, itching to begin preparations for her journey. She'd leave at first light before anyone else was awake.

Hold on, Thomas. I'm coming for you.

One day, Mrs. Lewis was going to learn how to gently place her jars of spices back on the rack after using them. Until then, Elijah never feared having no work to do. If nothing else, he'd have his weekly appointment fixing the shelf after she'd slammed a jar too hard and knocked the thing down.

The sound of quick footsteps coming toward the kitchen meant Mrs. Lewis was back to ask him if he was finished and why he didn't just fix it "good and proper," so it didn't fall down again. To which he'd have to respond, if she didn't wield her hand like a hammer, he wouldn't have to.

"I'm almost done, Mrs. Lewis," he called over his shoulder when he heard her enter the kitchen.

"Elijah, I need your help."

Elijah whipped around. Mrs. Wright loomed in the doorway, anxiously twisting her hands. Her skin had an ashen parlor to it, and genuine terror marred her beautiful features.

Elijah's stomach plummeted to his feet. "Yes, ma'am. What can I do to help?"

"I need you to bring my daughter home."

Elijah rubbed a hand over the back of his neck, trying to figure out how to respond. "Sorry, ma'am, but I don't know if that's a good idea. I haven't spoken to Henrietta in weeks and our last conversation was tense. Perhaps Matthew should pick her up."

"She ran away. Well, she left to rescue her cousin." Mrs. Wright extracted a crumpled note from her skirt pocket and handed it to Elijah.

His knees nearly buckled by the time he finished reading the letter. Henrietta had gone to Alabama. Alone. How could she be so reckless?

"How long ago did she leave? Where is she headed? I can be ready within the hour."

"I know I am partially to blame for this. I'm sorry, Elijah. Please find Henrietta and bring her home to me so I can apologize to her as well."

Now wasn't the time for heartfelt apologies, no matter how deserved. It was the time for action. Elijah tried his best to keep his tone level and keep his annoyance out of his voice. "I will. You have my word. Where can I find her?"

"Come with me. I will give you everything you need. She left sometime in the early hours of the morning."

Elijah followed behind her without hesitation. The next time he saw her, he was going to throttle Henrietta. Then hug her and make her promise to never pull such a harebrained stunt again. Rescuing Thomas alone from some place in Alabama.

Right then, a new thought dawned on Elijah. "How did Thomas end up in Alabama?"

"I believe at some point, he snuck off behind his father's back and joined the army. Which explains why my brother-in-law has been avoiding me as of late. I can only assume he got himself captured and thrown into a prison camp. Henrietta is heading there to confirm it is actually him and if so, rescue him somehow."

Sneaking off to join the army. Planning rescue missions from prison camps in the heart of the south. Elijah shook his head at the absurdity of it all. Members of this family must not think the laws of reality apply to them.

"How did Henrietta know about Thomas's capture? Did you tell his father?"

"No. Paul can't learn about this until they return. I can't tell you everything right now, but I'll give you what you need to know to catch her before she reaches her destiantion." Mrs. Wright entered her study with Elijah on her heels. She went to the bookshelf and pulled down a map. Unrolling it, she pointed to their location then traced her way down the map to Alabama.

"Henrietta doesn't have a visitation pass, so she'll probably travel to Kentucky, then sneak through Tennessee to avoid spending too much time behind enemy lines. I think I know the route she took, but she has a decent head start."

"You have my word, Mrs. Wright, that I will bring Henrietta home unharmed."

Mrs. Wright placed a hand on his cheek, an unwavering smile on her lips. "I know you will. That's why you're the only person I would trust to do this. Thank you. Now let's get you ready."

Taking the map with them, Elijah exited the study after Mrs. Wright.

Henrietta, wherever you are, please be careful. I'm coming for you, a stór. And this time I won't let you go.

Chapter Nineteen

The pounding of fast-approaching hoofbeats drove away the travel weariness plaguing Henrietta seconds before. She sat up in her saddle, all her senses on high alert. She guided her horse farther to the side of the road, bowing her head to hide her face under her wide-brimmed hat.

She'd made it into Alabama without any parlous incidents and only had a day's ride to her final destination. The universe wouldn't be so cruel as to send her trouble so close to the end of her journey. Hopefully, the stranger would continue on without a fuss. She leaned and dug into her saddlebag, gripping the handle of her Colt revolver, just in case they didn't.

"Henrietta, I know that's you," a strong, commanding voice, tinged with an Irish brogue, called out. "I know the shape of your body, even in men's clothing. Stop your horse right now."

Henrietta twisted in her saddle, her head jerking around to stare at the newcomer. She spoke in stunned disbelief, her voice rising several octaves. "Elijah? What on earth are you doing here?"

He galloped up beside her, then in a swift move, maneuvered his horse in front of her and brought it to a halt. Henrietta yanked on the reins of her horse, stopping it to keep it from colliding with his.

"Your mother sent me to bring you home, and I intend to make good on that promise."

"No."

"No?"

Henrietta almost wanted to laugh at his parroted response. It was his turn to feel the sting of rejection.

"I'm not going anywhere with you. I have a mission to complete. Now move out of my way." Henrietta guided her horse to the left, trying to steer it around Elijah, but he inched his horse back, blocking her retreat.

"Do you know how dangerous this is? If a Rebel scouting party finds you, they'll probably shoot you on the spot or worse. You need to come home with me right now."

Henrietta glared at Elijah, her furious snarl baring her clenched teeth. Her grip tightened on the reins until the leather straps chafed her delicate palms.

"Do not talk to me like I am an imbecile," she bit out in a low, venomous voice. "Yes, I know the dangers involved with what I'm doing. Thomas is being held in a prison camp, and neither you nor anyone else will stop me from helping him."

Elijah crossed his arms over his chest. "How? How will you, a lone woman, help him if he is being held in a camp by armed soldiers?"

"Men have been underestimating women for centuries. Ask Samson how that worked out for him. I have connections in Alabama. We'll figure something out."

"You mean the person who told you Thomas was in the camp in the first place?"

Henrietta's eyes narrowed suspiciously on him. Her horse pranced restlessly beneath her, reacting to the ire radiating off of her. "What do you know about that?"

"Your mother wouldn't tell me everything, but she knew you'd be coming here to talk to a man you consider a friend. She didn't give me a name, only the address, and the route she thought you'd take in hopes that I found you before you reached your intended destination."

"Go home, Elijah. As you said before, I can't keep relying on you to save me. I need to do this on my own."

Henrietta tried to guide her horse around Elijah's once more. A surprised yelp escaped her lips when he caught her off guard by snaking a strong arm around her waist and hauling her out of her saddle. He dropped her in front of him on his horse.

"I am not leaving here without you. I'm returning you to New York, where you will be safe like I promised your mother."

"How dare you touch me," Henrietta hissed.

Before she could stop herself, her hand shot out, slapping Elijah across the face.

She touched her fingers to her parted lips, her eyes stretched wide in bewilderment that she'd done such a thing. "I'm sorry. I don't know why I did that. I'm so sorry."

"No need to apologize. I deserved it. But it doesn't change the fact that you are coming home with me."

"No, I'm not."

Henrietta released an exasperated sigh. They were not going to agree on this, but she was not going to give in. Trying a new tactic, she took a calming breath and did her best to regain her composure.

She spoke in a soft, even voice and said, "You were right that night. I shouldn't have relied on you to save me. I should have saved myself. And that's what I'm doing now. The day those men attacked me, they took something from me. My sense of safety and belonging in the place I called home. I realized there is no 'safe place' for people that look like me in this country.

That's why I wanted to join the militia so badly. To be a part of the force that creates that safe place. But even that desire was misguided, because I thought I needed them in order to have an impact. I don't. This right here, going to rescue my cousin, will have an impact, even if only in his life. I don't need the militia to give what I do meaning. I don't need my mother's, or society's, approval of how I live my life. I just need to live it for me. To make myself happy and do what I can to create change, no matter how big or little. Now if you'll excuse me, I have somewhere I need to be."

Wordlessly, Elijah released Henrietta and helped her back into her saddle. She grabbed hold of the reins and steered her horse around him. This time, he didn't move to stop her. As she rode off, the slow, easy gate of Elijah's horse followed her.

"What are you doing?" she tossed over her shoulder, without looking back at him.

"Coming with you. I understand why you need to do this. And you should understand that I'm not leaving your side. I will help you accomplish whatever you decide to do."

"So be it."

They continued on in silence, both lost in their own thoughts. A tiny wisp of elation awoke inside of Henrietta at having Elijah by her side. She quickly tamped it down. Now wasn't the time or place for such emotions. They had a mission to complete, and not even her own heart would get in the way.

Elijah watched the way Henrietta swayed to the smooth rhythm of her horse's trot. He'd been staring at her back for the last day. Even when they'd stopped last night to rest, she'd lain out her sleep mat, then rolled onto her side, facing away from him.

At first, when she didn't speak to him, he'd wanted to give her the space he'd thought she needed. Twenty-four long, grueling hours later, he was on the verge of begging her to say something, anything, to him. There was nothing like the woman you love ignoring your very existence to make a man feel two feet tall.

Luckily, before he broke down, they rounded a bend and came upon a long drive leading to a large stately southern mansion. Elijah scanned the wide, open expanse of the plantation, in awe of the lush green grass and the well-kept white home with the wrap-around porch and navy-blue shutters.

What stunned him the most out of the entire scene was the throng of children with skin tones ranging from light brown to ebony, running around, laughing and playing as if they hadn't a care in the world. Elderly men and women were perched in rocking chairs, watching the children frolic. Thick, sprawling tree branches shielded them from the summer sun.

Off in the distance, men and women labored in the fields. Again, he was shocked to find some of them had skin as fair as his, and they labored side by side the colored men and women. There were no men on horses watching everyone to make sure they were working efficiently. In fact, a few men and women sat under the shade of the trees, fanning themselves with their hats while they rested.

Elijah had never been south of New York before, but this place didn't match the stories he'd heard about the nightmarish existence for slaves in the South. He beheld the happenings around him, mulling over the plethora of questions that fired off in his mind. He was so lost in thought that he almost didn't notice when they arrived in front of the two-story home, and Henrietta guided her horse to a stop.

Henrietta hopped down from her horse and marched up the front steps as if this place was as familiar to her as her own home. The front door opened, revealing an older white gentleman with mostly gray hair and a salt-and-pepper beard. He hooked his thumbs in the loops of his pants and smiled down at Henrietta with the pride and elation of a father welcoming their prodigal son home.

"Well, I'll be," he bellowed, his wide smile reaching all the way to his eyes. "Are these old eyes playing tricks on me, or is the most beautiful granddaughter a man could ever ask for standing in my yard?"

Granddaughter? Elijah's gaze bounced between the man on the porch and Henrietta.

This was her grandfather? A southern plantation owner in Alabama? More questions assaulted him as he followed a few steps behind her up the porch.

"Hello, Papa. Yes, those eyes are old, just like the rest of you. But they haven't started deceiving you yet."

"I thought not." He opened his arms for Henrietta, who happily ran into them. "It's good to see you. Been way too long. Thought I'd go to my grave only being able to remember you with pigtails."

They held each other in the drawn-out way of loved ones who hadn't seen each other in a considerable amount of time. Henrietta rested her head on his chest. He kissed the top of her head, hugging her tighter.

"Yes, far too long. I've missed you more than words can express."

Henrietta's grandfather gave her back two hearty pats. He pulled away enough to look her in the eyes. "So, what brings you down here? This wasn't part of our arrangement."

"The last bit of information you sent brought me here. I believe my cousin was one of the soldiers listed. I need to confirm that it's him, and if it is, I need your help to rescue him somehow. Whatever you can do for him will place me forever in your debt."

He chuckled, draping his arm over her shoulder, then steered her toward the front door. "Granddaughters can't be in their grandfather's debt. Come on inside and let's talk this through."

"Thank you."

"So, how's your ma? She still hates me? And who's this fella here?" he asked, pointing his thumb at Elijah.

"Please excuse me. Where are my manners?" Henrietta turned to Elijah, acknowledging him for the first time that day. "Elijah, this is my grandfather, Mr. George Henry Wright. Papa, this is Elijah Byrne."

"Irish, aye?" Her grandfather extended his hand to Elijah. They held onto each other's hands, shaking for longer than necessary. "You got a good grip. Did you watch out for my Henri on the trip down here?"

"Yes, sir. She disappeared without telling anyone. So, with her mother's help, I tracked her down. My intent was to take her home, but she was determined to come to see you, so I accompanied her the rest of the way."

Her grandfather nodded his approval. Letting go of Elijah's hand, he puffed out his chest and fixed him with an intimidating glower.

"You married, son?"

"No, sir."

"You will be before you return home. It ain't proper for an unmarried man and woman to be traipsing cross-country together. Folks will be waggin' their tongues about Henri for years. Her reputation will be ruined. You'll have to make amends for it."

"Papa!" Henrietta exclaimed, her hands on her hips. "Enough. Elijah doesn't have to marry me."

"'Course he does." Ignoring Henrietta, her grandfather quirked a suspicious eyebrow at Elijah. "Unless there is a reason he don't want to."

Henrietta tried to argue. "I'm the one that—"

"Yes sir, there's a reason I can't marry your granddaughter." Elijah spread his legs wide and clasped his hands behind his back. He kept his expression impassive.

Her grandfather mirrored Elijah's stoic posture. "Let's hear it, then."

"I don't have a penny to my name, sir. Back home, I work for Henrietta's family. Before that, I worked at the docks, barely scraping together enough to survive on. I have no formal education, and your granddaughter's reputation would be more tarnished by marrying me than not, sir."

"Son." Her grandfather shook his head, laughing to himself. "Did it ever occur to you that my granddaughter and her family have enough pennies for the both of you? I thought you were going to give a real reason. You a hard worker?"

"Yes, sir."

"You going to treat my grandbaby right?"

"Yes, sir."

"You'll give your life trying to protect her?"

"Yes, sir."

"Then, like I said, you'll be married before you leave here." He thumped Elijah on the back in a good-natured manner. "Can't believe Martha was fool enough to let y'all travel here unchaperoned. Y'all come on in this house so we can talk. It's hotter'in a witch's teet out here. I'm 'bout ready to pass out, standing on this here porch. I'll have MaryAnne bring us some lemonade."

"Don't I get a say in this?" Henrietta asked.

"Nope. Now stop your bellyaching and come on in."

Elijah followed behind a sulking Henrietta and her grandfather into the large house. His mind reeled with questions about what had just happened.

It looked like he would soon be Henrietta's husband. Too bad he couldn't believe such a glorious future would occur.

Chapter Twenty

Elijah walked toward the front door, headed to the porch in hopes of finding a cool breeze. New York summer days were hot, but Alabama heat made him wonder how people survived down here. What kind of person would choose to live in a place where the sun ran its scorching fingers over their bodies until they were burned and blistered?

Sleeping through the night had been nearly impossible. He'd waken up every so often in need of a towel to sop up the sweat pouring down his face and body in heavy rivulets. Even now in the early hours of the morning, it wouldn't be hard to convince him that the temperature was two hundred degrees. He couldn't wait to return to New York, and its reasonable weather.

He stepped outside and immediately closed his eyes and held his face up to the wind. There wasn't much of a breeze, but at least he didn't feel as if he were sitting in an oven like a chicken volunteering for roasting.

"Come on over here and grab you a class of this here sweet tea."

Elijah opened his eyes then turned to look at Mr. Wright. The older gentleman sat in a chair, a glass of ice-cold tea in one hand and a handkerchief in the other. He brought the small piece of cloth to his forehead and dabbed at his excessive sweat.

"Good morning, sir," Elijah said, with a nod to the other man. "I beg your pardon. Didn't mean to intrude." He took a step back, ready to retreat back into the house.

"Nonsense. Come on out here and sit." He pointed to the pitcher of tea with tiny remnants of ice floating at the top and the empty set of glasses beside it. "Go on and pour yourself a glass. MaryAnne makes the best tea on this side of the Mississippi."

"Thank you, sir." Elijah took the seat next to Mr. Wright and poured himself a glass of tea.

The cold, sweet, maple-colored liquid filled his mouth and flowed over his tongue, causing an explosion of toe-curling ecstasy to spread through his body. He sighed in contentment, relaxing and sagging further into his chair. Mr. Wright was right.

"You're right, sir. Best sweet tea I've ever had in my entire life."

"Umm-hmm. Henri still sleeping?"

"Yes, sir."

"Good."

They settled into a comfortable silence, sipping tea and occupying themselves with their own thoughts. Despite the excruciating heat, Elijah had to admit there was a certain beauty to this place.

"You love my granddaughter," Mr. Wright finally spoke.

Elijah continued to focus on the landscape in front of him. It was a statement, not a question, but he answered anyway.

"Yes sir, I do."

"I can see it in the way you look at her. Like you want to hold her up high on your shoulders and carry her above all the evil in the world. I used to look at her grandmother the same way."

That aroused Elijah's full curiosity. He wasn't on good enough terms with Henrietta to ask her about her family history, so all last night, he'd pondered the possibilities to himself.

"Would it be rude of me to ask what happened between the two of you?"

Mr. Wright remained silent, his jaw working and hand flexing on his glass. Elijah waited patiently, hoping he would answer. From the haunted, distant look in his eyes, it didn't seem as if the story would be a pleasant one.

"I was a greedy fool. Her name was Evangeline Martha Turner. My Eva. She was a slave on a plantain near mine when we was growing up. She was the handmaid to her owner's daughter, Rebecca Jennings. We'd see each other in passing and at different events. She was breathtaking. Everything she did was graceful, from drinking water to sweeping the floor. And her smile." His eyes glazed over with a dreamy, faraway look. His own lips spread into a spirited grin. "I swear she always had a smile on her face, but when I came 'round, it took on a magical quality. Like she'd been waiting all day to see me, and now that she had, she was good and truly happy."

That didn't sound like a terrible story. Elijah had been expecting something with a bit more tragedy.

"So, you purchased her and set her free?" He chimed in, guessing the ending of Mr. Wright's story. "That's why Henrietta and her mother live the way they do."

"No, although I wish I had. I married Rebecca, knowing that Eva would come along. I would leave flowers and little love notes in her room. At first, she asked me to stop. She didn't want to disrespect her mistress. Being the devilish bastard that I am, I kept on pursuing her. Kept on charming her until she gave in. We started an affair and not long after she got with child. She told me to leave her alone after that. She thought God would punish us for our sins. I told her that kind of thinking was hogwash. 'God wants us to be happy,' I told her. 'And you make me happy.' But she still wouldn't let me touch her after that.

Not too long later, Rebecca ended up carrying as well, but it was hard on her. She was always so sick and could barely keep anything down. Eva said it was our doing. We'd invited the bad spirits in with what we'd done. She stopped eating. Drove me out my mind watching her starve herself. She finally started eating enough to stay alive when I told her refusing to eat would kill the baby, and that would add murder to her list of sins. And she didn't want to make God mad by murdering a baby. I had to watch the woman I love wither away right in front of me. Eva died not long after Martha was born. She was so weak she couldn't even nurse her. Rebecca and the baby died a few months later in the birthing process."

Elijah sat there for a moment, staring into his glass. Any words of comfort would fall short. How did one respond to another's confession of their greatest sins and deepest regrets?

"I'm sorry for your losses. I can't imagine that type of pain."

"Eva was right." Mr. Wright's chin quivered, but his eyes remained dry. He cleared his throat before continuing. "I brought all that upon myself with my greed and selfishness. I wanted Eva, but I wanted to preserve my reputation and have a proper Southern bride to take to parties and dinners. If I could do it all over, I would do it differently."

"At least you did right by Martha. Again, if it's not too intrusive, why doesn't she speak to you anymore?"

"As soon as she was born, I had her freedom papers drawn up, but I never claimed her in public as my own. Darn stupid since she looks just like me." Mr. Wright shook his head. "Anyway, I sent her to the best boarding schools up North and made sure she had everything she ever wanted. She was my last link to her mother. My light in the darkness.

Every time she smiled at me and said she loved me, a tiny piece of my guilt fell away. Then not long after her eighteenth birthday, she was visiting from school, and one of the maids who'd been good friends with Martha told her the truth. Everything about Eva, Rebecca, and me. She refused to talk to me after that. Said she hated me. The last piece of my heart died that day."

Elijah leaned forward, resting his elbows on his knees, and swirling the tea in the glass. Wow! There were so many layers to that story. So many things to digest. And so many lives destroyed. He couldn't even imagine the burden of guilt Mr. Wright must carry.

Processing what he'd heard a little further, a new question came to Elijah. "How did you and Henrietta get to know each other?"

"Even after she stopped talking to me, I continued to deposit money into an account for Martha. It sat there for years because she refused to accept anything from me. Then she met and married Samuel. I reached out to him, telling him who I was, what I'd done. Then I convinced him to start using the money. We kept in contact, although I'm sure he never told Martha. One day he asked me to visit him in New York. He brought Henri with him. She was about ten at the time. The most beautiful thing I ever saw. She reminded me of Eva so much. Still does. Samuel arranged a handful of meetings between us before he died. I taught Henri how to write coded messages so we could write letters to each other without her mother knowing."

"A skill she has now decided to put into practice in service of the Union Army. I still can't believe she had an entire plan to join the Black Militia for Union Victory." Elijah placed his glass back on the small table between their chairs. He'd become privy to so many secrets and hidden plans last night, he now looked at Henrietta in an entirely different light. "And I can't believe you helped her. Why?"

"Because she's all the family I have left. I'd do anything for her. Plus, I figured if she's as bullheaded as her mama, she'd do what she wanted, whether I helped her or not. At least this way, I can be there to protect her if anything goes wrong."

"Good point."

Mr. Wright shifted in his seat, facing Elijah, and fixing him with a stern look. "Your reasons for not wanting to marry Henri may be different than mine with her grandma, but it's foolery all the same. Don't let anything get between you and the woman you love. The good book says something like, 'there is no fear in love. Perfect love casteth out fear.' Don't deny what's meant for you because you're afraid. Have a little faith in yourself and her. She's a good woman. She'll stand by your side no matter what if you treat her right. Besides, thinking his woman is above his station helps keep a man grateful and his eye from wandering, if you catch my meaning."

They both chuckled at the last portion of Mr. Wright's speech. Elijah couldn't argue with him there. The mere thought of Henrietta catching him even sneezing in another woman's direction made him nervous.

"Wise words. Thank you, sir."

"Umm-hmm. And remember, you ever step out of line, I've no problems puttin' two bullets in your sorry hide."

"I'll never forget it."

"I know you won't."

Mr. Wright reached over and gave Elijah's back two quick pats. As they settled back into their chairs, Elijah noticed a wagon ambling down the long drive.

"Looks like the team is here," Mr. Wright said, rising from his chair. "Come on, let's wake Henri up and get this thing started."

"Yes, sir."

Sitting on a porch in Alabama sipping the best sweet tea he'd ever tasted. Being challenged to swallow down his fear and confessing his love for Henrietta. Taking part in secret operations to rescue a captured soldier. The last few days had been full of experiences that Elijah never thought he'd have.

If he ever did muster the courage to tell her how he felt, if nothing else, he could guarantee life with Henrietta would be anything but ordinary.

Chapter Twenty-One

Five pairs of eyes peered at Henrietta as she entered her grandfather's study. Elijah, her grandfather, and three new additions. She'd done her best to freshen up and get dressed as quickly as possible, so as not to keep them waiting long.

"Good morning, everyone. I apologize for my tardiness."

Henrietta acknowledged each person in turn. Various forms of "good morning" replied to her greeting.

"Now that everyone is here, we can get started. Take a seat, Henri." Her grandfather motioned to the only available chair in the room, next to the other woman, then waited for her to be seated. "I'll go ahead and get the introductions out of the way. This here is Silas, and his son, Jim. They work for me. And this is Sarah. She works for Mrs. Williams. This lovely young lady is my granddaughter, Henrietta, and that's her man, Elijah."

"Wonderful to meet all of you," Henrietta said, ignoring her grandfather's comments about Elijah being her man. She'd stopped being mad at him at some point along the last leg of their journey here. Now she didn't speak to him because she simply didn't know what to say.

"Pleasure," Elijah added.

The others nodded their heads and replied with similar cordial acknowledgments.

"I've confirmed that your cousin, Thomas, is indeed in the prison camp. This little group here is going to break him out."

"Break him out?" Elijah repeated, shock over the declaration evident in his pinched expression. "How? Do you really think we can pull off such a thing?"

Her grandfather hooked his thumbs around his suspenders, meeting Elijah's unsure gaze with a confident one. "It won't be easy, but it's not impossible. Thomas is being held at Camp Blake over in Baldwin. The soldiers know me and Sarah already. I bring her over there to tend the ailing soldiers. Union and Confederate alike. I tell 'em I'm doing it on behalf of her mistress, and her bleeding heart for all men. Really, Sarah's memory is better than anyone I ever met." He tipped his head to her, a proud grin on his lips. "She helps me gather the information to pass along to my contacts."

Elijah scooted closer to the edge of his chair. "So, you deliver intelligence to several different people?"

"Of course. Damn Yanks seem to think this war is a game of every man for himself. They hold on to intelligence and don't pass it up the chain. Sometimes, good information is never acted on. I figure if I pass the information along to a few people, maybe someone will make use of it."

"Makes sense." Elijah nodded in agreement.

"That all sounds like a good cover, Papa. What do you need us to do?"

Her grandfather perused the group. He pointed at each person as he listed their instructions. "Elijah is going to pose as a doctor. Sarah will give him the basics of what he needs to do and say. Henri and Sarah, you two will pretend to be his assistants. I'll do what I normally do and jabber with the soldiers. Keep them occupied." He looked squarely at

Henrietta and said, "Make sure to tend a few other soldiers first; don't go straight to Thomas. Once you do get to him, tell him to pretend to be dead." He looked away, scratching his bearded chin. In a solemn voice, he added, "I hate to say this, but I don't think it will be a hard sell. I heard he got shot in battle before being captured. The wound is infected, and he ain't doing so good. They keep him with the others they're waiting on to die."

Henrietta's hand flew to her chest, her head jerking back. "When did this happen? Have you all been treating him?"

Sarah leaned over and touched a gentle hand to Henrietta's shoulder. "He came into the camp several weeks ago," she said, her voice filled with sympathy. "I've done the best I can for him, but my supplies are limited. If it weren't for his youth and prior good health, I don't think he would have made it as long as he has."

Henrietta took note of the other woman's French accent. How odd. Despite her grandfather's introduction stating Sarah worked for Mrs. William, Henrietta understood the unspoken truth: she was a slave. Why did a slave from Alabama have a French accent? Henrietta pushed those thoughts to the back of her mind. Her curiosity would have to be satisfied another day.

For now, her focus needed to be solely on rescuing Thomas.

Henrietta covered Sarah's hand with her own. "Thank you for all that you've done for him." Focusing back on her grandfather, she asked, "What do we need to do after that?"

"The soldiers are kept in a holding pen made from twenty-foot wooden logs. Elijah will confirm Thomas's death, and then Jim and Silas will come over and drag him out of the pen and put him in the pit with the other dead bodies. He'll have to stay there till nightfall when Elijah, Jim, and Silas can come back and get him out."

Henrietta blanched. She swallowed several times, choking down the urge to vomit. "How horrible," she said when she finally trusted herself to speak without purging the few morsels of cheese and bread that she'd nibbled on for breakfast.

"I can't lie and say it ain't. But it's the best chance we have of getting him out of there."

"I know. It's just..." Poor Thomas. He'd have to sit in that pit, surrounded by dead men, smelling their revolting stench for hours. The idea of it filled Henrietta with anguish. Her chest began to heave the longer she thought about it.

Try as she might, she couldn't pull a breath into her air-deprived lungs.

"Look at me, *a stór*. Look at me," Elijah said to Henrietta. He came over and kneeled in front of her, then touched a finger under her chin to lift her eyes to meet his. "We're going to rescue Thomas and bring him home safely. That's what's most important. Whatever we need to do to make that happen, we'll do."

"You're right." Henrietta nodded vigorously, choking back the tears stinging her eyes. Holding Elijah's hand for emotional support, she faced her grandfather again. "When do we leave?"

"Tonight. We'll go right before dusk, so he doesn't have to lay in the pit for long."

"All right. I'll be ready."

"Good. I've got a few things around the estate to take care of. Everyone be back here two hours before dusk."

"Yes, sir, boss man," Silas said. "We're gonna head home for a while. The missus needs Jim's help in the garden before we go."

"I need to leave as well," Sarah added. "Mrs. Williams is taking care of my daughter for me. I need to update her about our plans."

"Sounds good. See you all again tonight." Henrietta's grandfather rose from his chair.

"Henrietta, I'm going to drag these tired bones upstairs. I'll be back down later."

"Yes, Papa. I'll be ready tonight."

"I know you will." He patted her hands, then followed everyone else out.

The room emptied, except for Henrietta and Elijah. They must have had the same idea. Henrietta wanted to speak with Elijah, although she still hadn't worked out exactly what she wanted to tell him. He looked as if he had something he wished to say as well, but something held him back.

They stared at each other, eyes meeting and never shifting away. Henrietta folded her hands in front of herself, then let them fall and hang at her sides. Nervous energy fluttered through her, winding its way into her chest, making her heart vibrate like the flapping wings of a hummingbird.

Elijah rubbed a hand over the back of his neck. "May we talk for a moment?"

"Yes."

"It means 'my treasure.'"

"What does?"

"*A stór*. It means 'my treasure.'" Elijah stepped forward and took both of Henrietta's hands in his. He smiled when she didn't pull away. "You are my greatest treasure, Henrietta.

My safe place in a world that has let me down again and again. You look at me like I'm a man. Not a worthless immigrant."

"Because you are, Elijah. You are! I need to apologize to you. The day those women came and found us together, it exposed an ugliness in my heart. I didn't want them gossiping about me because I was with you. I was too much of a coward to face the opinions of others. I'm sorry. Please forgive me."

Elijah brought her right hand to his lips and kissed her palm. "Already forgiven. That day exposed my own self-doubts, but now I see that's a good thing. It will make sure I never forget how lucky I am to have you. How lucky I am that I am spending the rest of my days making you happy. I love you. I love you more than I've ever loved another person."

He lifted her hands to his lips and kissed each of her fingers in turn. "I don't have a ring to give you right now. I wasn't expecting to have the courage to do this. But I love you too much not to have you in my life for the rest of my days. Henrietta Catherine Wright, will you do me the honor and privilege of being my wife?"

Henrietta gasped, her hands flying to cover her mouth. "Yes! Yes, I'll be your wife."

She gripped the front of his shirt and pulled Elijah in for a passionate kiss. She kissed him with all the love, yearning, hopes, and dreams she had for them. She made promises of forever with her lips.

He'd spoken of being lucky to have her. She was equally as lucky to have him. Joy, elation, and peace surged through her heart, making her want to announce her happiness to anyone who crossed her path.

Elijah lifted her off the ground and spun her in a small circle. "I love you. I love you. I love you," he said between kisses.

Henrietta stroked the side of his handsome face. "And I love you."

Elijah placed her back on her feet, kissed her one last time, then took a step away. "I have to let you go for now. Too many more of your sweet kisses and I'll really have to answer to your grandfather for ruining you. He mentioned something about having bullets waiting for me," he said with a lopsided grin.

"All right." Henrietta poked out her bottom lip in mock disappointment. "I guess I can find something to do with myself until later. I still have a lot of catching up to do with my grandfather."

"Excellent." Elijah kissed her forehead. "Have fun. I will be around if you need me."

"Same for me."

"I love you, *a stór*."

"I love you too, Elijah Byrne."

Henrietta walked to the door, leaving Elijah standing with his hands in his pockets. Right before she reached to open it, he bounded up behind her and placed one last kiss on her neck. Before she could do anything in response, he opened the door, then shoved her through it, closing it behind her. Henrietta giggled at the sheer silliness of it all. She had a feeling there would be many more such moments to look forward to for the rest of her life.

Chapter Twenty-Two

Vivid yellows, reds, and oranges streaked across the early evening sky. Henrietta watched the downy white clouds sail lazily across the endless expanse of color as if they were trying to enjoy the beauty of the natural masterpiece. It wasn't the same as the sunset Elijah had shown her in New York, but it was very similar.

Perhaps the difference had nothing to do with the sky, but the emotions she felt while observing each. That day, words like cherished, enamored, and fascinated would have been apt descriptions for the basis of her mood.

Today, a sobering determination held the majority of share of her emotional state.

Henrietta sat in her grandfather's wagon, quietly swaying with the bumps and dips in the dirt road. Elijah perched on the wagon bench with her grandfather while she huddled with Sarah, Silas, and Jim in the wagon bed. The tall wooden walls of the prison camp's holding area soon came into view. It was probably her imagination running wild, but Henrietta could almost see the shadowy black hand of death looming in this place.

As they came closer, her grandfather waved at the nearby soldiers. He pulled the wagon to a stop in front of the prisoner's holding area and smiled at the two guards outside the gate.

He hopped down from the wagon, Elijah doing the same. They strolled over to the guards, then her grandfather tipped his hat to the two men. "Hey, Pete, Jack. How's it goin'?"

"Same old, same old," Pete said in a casual tone. "Yanks complaining about not having enough to eat. Our men complaining about not having enough to eat. And we're forced to stand out here in the hot sun all day, listening to it."

Her grandfather chuckled at the other man's complaints. "I don't envy your situation."

"Neither do I," Pete replied with a snort. He pointed at the wagon. "What you got going on over here?"

"I brought a whole work crew." He jabbed his thumb in Elijah's direction. "Complete with a doctor to take a look at the prisoners, and any of your men, who need him."

"Gentleman," Elijah said tipping his hat.

Jack spit a long stream of brown liquid on the ground, clearing space in his mouth to talk. "We sure do 'ppreciate you two taking the time. Some of the men been complaining 'bout bug bites and the like."

"We don't have much in the way of medicine and supplies," Elijah said, immersing himself in the role of a doctor. "But we'll do our best to make do and help as many men as possible."

Henrietta's grandfather pointed at the wagon. "And Jim and Silas there are gonna help out with any labor y'all might need doing. Digging ditches and whatnot."

"Again, we sure do appreciate you. Y'all come on in." Jack leaned back and looked at the men at the top of the guard towers. He spun his arm in a circular motion, then shouted, "Open the gate."

Tipping their hats one last time at the guards, Elijah and Henrietta's grandfather traipsed back to the wagon. The heavy wooden gate creaked and moaned in protest as it slowly opened.

Taking up the reigns, Elijah guided the wagon
into the prisoner holding area.

The stench of unwashed bodies, fecal matter,
and disease assaulted Henrietta's nose as soon as
they passed through the gate. The odors were so
pungent she could taste them. Her stomach
roiled, constricting until she wasn't sure if it
would collapse in on itself. Henrietta covered
her nose to keep from gagging.

Elijah parked the wagon, and everyone
silently got out. They jumped down, landing
with a slight splash in the foul, swampy mud,
and God knew what else.

"Y'all know what to do," her grandfather
whispered, then walked off back toward Jack
and Pete.

Henrietta walked next to Sarah through the
sea of men. Some peeked at them curiously;
most didn't even take the time to move an
extended leg out of the way, expecting the
women to move around them.

Dull, haunting expressions rested on
everyone's faces. Even the men in better physical
health looked as if they had battled death and
weren't sure if they enjoyed coming out
victorious.

Following Sarah's lead, Henrietta knelt in
front of a solider with blistering red skin. Like

many of the others, he sat in the large, open area without much protection from the scorching summer sun.

"Hello, sir," Sarah said in a soothing voice as if she were talking to a wild animal poised to strike. "My name is Sarah, and this is Henrietta. We've come to attend your injuries. It appears you might have a case of sun poisoning. May we assist you?"

The soldier cut his eyes to Sarah, then Henrietta. Suspicion laced his weary gaze as if he wondered if they were tricking him—if they were really there to finish him off.

"We don't promise to work miracles, but we can help relieve your suffering," Henrietta added, hoping the truth about the limits of their abilities would put him at ease.

"All right," the young man croaked through dried lips. "Do what you can."

Sarah nodded, then went through her sack of supplies to scrounge up what she needed. Henrietta assisted where she could, her gaze occasionally wandering over the other nearby soldiers. Her heart froze, dying a gut-wrenching death, when she finally saw Thomas.

His formerly youthful, mahogany face now had a sickly, ashen paleness to it. He lay on his side, his hands tucked beneath his head, and his unblinking, glazed, red-rimmed eyes stared off in the distance as if he were afraid to close them for fear of nightmares once again plaguing him.

Henrietta forced herself to look away. To turn her back on her suffering cousin for now, so as not to ruin the plan that would save him in the long run. She'd never done anything so painful in her entire life.

She handed Sarah the ingredients and tools she asked for, silently wailing her sorrow inside.

When they'd seen to enough of the other soldiers and the time came for them to go to Thomas, Henrietta walked on wobbling knees to her cousin's side.

"Thomas. Thomas, it's me, Henrietta," she whispered to him.

Thomas finally blinked several times and turned his head toward her. "Retta? Is it really you?"

She took his hand in hers, trying her best not to squeeze it too hard. "Yes. It's me, Thomas." She swiped at a stubborn tear that forced its ways down her face. She motioned to Sarah. "This is Sarah. We've come to rescue you."

A little of his brightness dimmed again. He withdrew his hand from hers and tucked it under his armpits. "How? Anyone who crosses that fence is shot on sight." He said then pointed to the short, basic fence around the perimeter of the holding pen. "No one escapes from here. We can't even get close enough to try."

Henrietta watched her cousin leer at her as if she was the enemy. Like she'd cruelly dangled a branch of hope in front of him, only to snatch it away. If she weren't confident in her ability to make good on her promise of rescue, his mistrust would have stung.

Before she could answer him, a violent cough racked Thomas's body. He curled into himself and covered his mouth with his dirt-smeared fist. Henrietta rubbed his back until he settled again.

"That cough sounds nasty. Here, drink this." Sarah cradled his head and lifted him into enough of a sitting position for him to drink the liquid in the glass bottle she held to his lips.

He slurped it up, occasionally dribbling some down his chin, until the bottle was empty.

"Now, listen carefully, Thomas," Henrietta whispered when he settled back on his side. "I need you to do everything I say, so we can get you out of here. After Sarah and I walk away, you need to pretend to be dead. That man there is with us." She pointed to Elijah, tending to the other soldiers a few feet away. "He's pretending to be a doctor. We'll send him over to you, and he'll pronounce you dead. Then, our other men will haul you out to the dead man's pit."

Thomas's eyes went wide. If he had the energy, Henrietta was sure he would have gotten up and run away. "The dead man's pit? I don't want to touch dead bodies. The smell alone will be enough to turn my stomach."

"You don't have a choice." Henrietta tried to keep an even tone. To be sympathetic to his concerns, but time was running out. The sun was setting and their window of opportunity was closing. "This is what needs to be done so we can get you home. You want to go home, don't you?"

"Yeah."

"Then do as I say."

He stayed silent for several seconds. With a reluctant sigh, he nodded his head. "Yes, ma'am."

"Once they put you in the pit, you have to stay there until we come to get you. We'll be back as soon as the sun sets."

"How am I supposed to lay with a bunch of dead bodies without tossing my guts?"

"Take these and put them in your nose." Sarah handed him two fragrant cotton plugs. Then she gave him another small vile of liquid. "And after we leave, drink this. It will slow down your breathing and make you very relaxed. You'll hardly notice anything."

Thomas grabbed Henrietta's hand again and gave it a tight squeeze. "Thank you. I mean it. Thank you for coming to get me. I never should have disobeyed my father. He was right. There's no glory in this."

Henrietta stroked the side of his dirt-covered face, then kissed his cheek. She gave him her best smile, although due to the circumstances, it most likely fell short of containing true cheerfulness. "Hush up and save all that 'he's right' stuff to tell your father when you see him. It'll be soon, I promise."

"I believe you. Thank you."

"All right. Remember the plan. We'll see you again later."

Henrietta and Sarah stood and moved on the next solider. As they passed Elijah, she tapped his shoulder, signaling the time to carry out the next phase of the plan. When he finished up with the man he was working on, Elijah went over to Thomas, who laid motionless in the same position Henrietta and Sarah had left him.

From then on, everything went off without a hitch. Elijah went to Pete and Jack, who laughed and smoked fresh, fat cigars courtesy of her grandfather, and announced Thomas's death.

They were in such good moods that they didn't make a fuss when her grandfather told them to let Silas and Jim take care of the body, so they could continue their talk.

Henrietta watched the two men carry her cousin's limp body through the gate into the woods to the mass grave of countless other dead men.

It's not real. It's not real.

She chanted that truth over and over to keep herself grounded in reality.

This nightmare would all be over soon. She, Thomas, and Elijah would be safely back in New York, and this entire experience would be behind them. Although the scars of it would stay on her heart for the rest of her life.

Chapter Twenty-Three

One thing Henrietta would always remember from this journey was that Alabama did nothing in half measure. The darkness was so thick she felt as if she were in a void of nothingness. If it weren't for the crickets and other nocturnal creatures chanting their nighttime rituals, Henrietta might have been convinced she'd somehow lost her vision.

She sat on the driver's bench of the wagon, waiting for Jim and Elijah to emerge from the darkness, carrying Thomas between them. The restlessness of her bouncing leg increased the longer she waited. They'd disappeared into the woods what felt like hours ago. Surely, they'd been able to find Thomas by now.

What she wouldn't give to have someone else waiting with her. Someone to whisper to and take her mind off the endless waiting. Her grandfather awaited them at home, and Silas had escorted Sarah back to her mistress.

Henrietta squinted into the woods, straining to see or hear anyone coming towards her. Finally, the crunches of twigs and leaves under heavy feet echoed from the woods. Henrietta looked at the night sky and sent up a word of gratitude. The men were finally back, and they could get out of here. She jumped down from the wagon and took a few steps forward to meet them.

At the last minute, something dawned on her. The noise was coming from the wrong direction. Jim and Elijah had gone to the left. The rustling came from the right. Before she could run back to the wagon and hide, a solider stumbled from between the trees, nearly colliding with Henrietta in his clumsy state.

He reeked of alcohol and tobacco. His heavy, half-closed, glassy eyes confirmed his state of inebriation. He'd probably wandered out here in search of a place to relieve himself.

When he finally looked up and saw Henrietta, he scratched his messy mop of hair, staring as if trying to decide if she were real, or a figment of his drunken imagination. "Who are you," he asked, clearly choosing the former rather than the latter conclusion. "What are you doing out here?"

"I... Um..."

He took a bumbling step forward, then stopped to regain his balance. Now steady, he once again looked at Henrietta, then turned to the wagon. "You're trespassing," he slurred. "You a spy or something? Help!" he shouted before she could answer. "Spy! Spy!"

Henrietta scanned the area for something heavy to hit the man with. She dashed back to the wagon but found nothing of use. His insistent hollering was going to have the entire Rebel army crashing down on her head. As she continued to search the surrounding woods, the man's screams were suddenly cut off, followed by a loud "Oof" and the thud of something solid hitting the ground.

Picking up the first decent-sized branch she saw, Henrietta crept back over to the solider. He was passed out cold on the ground. She looked up at the man standing over him, a revolver in his hand gripped like a club. He wore the double-breasted gray coat of a Confederate officer.

The only thing that kept her from dissolving into hysterical panic was the short colored woman tucked into the man's side. His arm was wrapped around her protectively, and she clung to him like he was her lifeline.

Henrietta stared at the odd pair, not knowing what to say.

"My name is Captain Andrews. I won't hurt you." He slowly lowered the hand holding the gun, then holstered the weapon at his side. "I need your help." He inclined his head to the woman at his side. "This is Olivia. She's been under my care for the past five months, but she isn't safe here anymore. I need you to take her with you. Make sure she makes it safely North. Keep her safe until I can come to get her. Whatever expenses you incur for her care, I will reimburse, but this should at least handle most of her basic expenses." He pulled out a banknote and handing it to Henrietta.

They all stood there, Henrietta unsure of what to do and the other two people waiting for her response. She'd come to rescue Thomas and now was faced with the possibility of taking on another charge. Getting back to New York would be difficult as it was. Ignoring the banknote for a moment, she focused on the beautiful ebony-skinned woman.

"Hello, Olivia. It is a pleasure to meet you. My name is Henrietta."

"Ma'am," she said in a soft, almost musical voice.

"It would be my honor to help you, if that is what you want." Henrietta held out her hand to the other woman. Olivia's eyes dropped to her outstretched hand, then up to the captain.

He nodded, encouraging her to accept.

"Don't worry, I will take good care of her."

Eyes still on the captain, Oliva asked, "How will you find me?"

Captain Andrews said nothing. Henrietta watched him. She could see his mind working. He didn't want to lie to Olivia or give her false promises yet wanted her to be reassured so she would move on to freedom.

"He can find you at my home," Henrietta answered, stepping in to relieve the captain of the burden of lying. "The Wright family residence in Brooklyn, New York."

"Thank you," the captain replied, inclining his head in gratitude.

In a moment so fast Henrietta barely saw it, the captain unholstered his gun and aimed it in the direction of the rustling of new intruders coming through the woods. Elijah and Jim emerged from the darkness, each with one of

Thomas's arms slung around their neck as they carried him between them. They stopped cold seeing the captain and his gun pointed in their direction.

"It's okay," Henrietta said, holding up her hands and stepping between the two opposing parties. "They are with me. And he is a friend."

"Who are you?" Elijah asked, his voice stony.

"Captain Gabriel Andrews."

"He wants us to take Olivia with us back up North. And we'd be delighted to do so."

Henrietta could tell Elijah wanted to argue. At the very least, he wanted to further discuss the folly of taking a woman under a Rebel officer's care with them. For all, they knew it could all be some sort of trap. But time did not leave them much room for such debates and inquiries.

"Well, let's be off then."

They all climbed into the wagon and quickly pulled off, leaving Captain Andrews to watch their departure.

Henrietta gently lifted Thomas's head, careful not to wake him, while Sarah fluffed his pillow. He'd been out for three days so far. The doctor said the infection had taken its toll, but with medicine, rest, plenty of fluids, and time for his body to heal, he would survive with minimal after-effects.

Placing him back on the pillows, she tucked the blankets around him, doing her best to keep him comfortable. Henrietta smiled at Olivia when she entered the bedroom, carrying a pitcher of cool water.

"Thank you, Olivia," she said in a pleasant voice.

"The least I can do. Thank you again for taking me with you."

"We'd never leave someone in need behind." Henrietta rubbed a friendly hand over Olivia's arm, then took the pitcher of water. "Besides, I must admit I was rather intrigued by the entire situation. A Confederate captain bringing a colored woman to me, asking for me to take her up North." Her eyes fell to Olivia's rounded belly. "And she's pregnant to boot. These are the types of stories so farfetched one can't fathom them to make them up."

Henrietta and Sarah chuckled, and a small smile pulled on the corner of Olivia's lips.

"May I ask how you came to be in his care?" Sarah asked.

Olivia dropped her eyes to the ground and twisted the fabric of her skirt around her fingers. "The baby ain't his, if that's what you're thinking.

He found me about five months back when I was running away from my old master. There was a party of soldiers patrolling, and he was with them. He took the uniform off a dead man and made me put it on. Tucked my hair under a hat and told the other men I was a man, and I wasn't to be harmed. When we got back to the camp, he took some criticism for it, but he kept me with him in his tent. Said I was to be his personal servant. I've been there ever since until y'all came along, and he gave me to you."

There was more to the story. Henrietta could sense it, but she wouldn't pry. At least not yet.

"Well, you will be safe with me until he comes to fetch you. Have you ever been to New York?"

"No, ma'am."

"I think you'll like it. There are so many places I want to show you. I'm a teacher, so if you ever wish to learn to read and write, I am happy to help you learn."

Olivia lifted her head a little higher, her chest puffing with pride. "Gabriel taught me."

"I'm sorry," Henrietta said, her cheeks warming at her blunder. "I made an assumption. Please forgive me."

Olivia waved off the apology. "It's all right. Before I met him, your assumption would have been true. He helped me in more ways than one."

Henrietta hadn't missed the way Olivia had called the captain by his first name. Or the affection shimmering in her eyes whenever she spoke of him. She dared to think Olivia might love him.

Yes, one day, she was going to have to pry the entire story out of her.

"So he did. And what about you, Sarah?" Henrietta asked, equally curious of the slave with a French accent who had helped her save her cousin. "Have you ever been to New York?"

"I don't know. I don't remember anything from my life before I woke up in chains two years ago."

Henrietta touched a hand to her throat. The poor woman. That must have been such a traumatic experience.

"Do you know how you lost your memory?" Henrietta asked. "An accident of some sort, maybe?"

"No, I don't. It's like I woke up one day in this life. I do have this strange feeling I'm not meant to be here. Like this isn't actually the life I was born to live."

"Do you want to come with us back to New York? Such a large party may be difficult to sneak across the country, but nothing is impossible."

Sarah gave her a sad smile, shaking her head. "Your offer is very kind, but no thank you. I have a young daughter, Hope. My mistress has promised that when she dies, there is a provision in her will to set us free. I want my daughter to have true freedom. To be able to walk down the street without worrying about a slave catcher snatching her up and shipping her back here. My mistress is strict but fair. I can spend the few years she has left, if even that long, with her for Hope's sake."

Henrietta's heart broke for this woman and her child. The love of a mother knew no bounds. She could only imagine how hard it would be to turn down a chance at immediate freedom to give your child the opportunity to know both freedom and peace. That took true strength.

"I understand," Henrietta said, in admiration.

Olivia ran a hand over her protruding belly. "I never thought of being anybody's mama. It still feels weird every time I feel the baby moving. I don't know you, but I can tell you love your child very much. I hope I'm able to love mine like that."

"You will," Sarah assured her. "No matter how or why that child came to be, it's a part of you. It may be hard, but your love for the child will win over your hate for the father."

Olivia nodded, understanding not only what Sarah said, but what she didn't say.

Oh, my word.

Henrietta was struck momentarily speechless by that powerful statement. These women had suffered so much, and yet continued to live, to strive for something better for themselves and those they loved. She said a silent prayer to be at least half the woman they were someday.

"We should let him rest," Sarah said, gathering up the dirty clothes they'd used to clean Thomas.

Henrietta and Olivia followed her lead out the door. This journey had been full of powerful lessons Henrietta would never forget. Walking with these women, a new idea for the future came to mind. She couldn't wait to find Elijah and tell him.

Elijah sat on the front porch. Sipping a glass of what he still had to agree was the best sweet tea he'd ever tasted, he watched the clouds float across the sky. The exuberant grin that seemed to be the default setting of his mouth these days slowly grew when he heard the front door open.

Cinnamon and her.

"Hello, my love," Henrietta's sweet voice called out to him.

"Hello, a stór."

She kissed his cheek, then sat in the chair next to him. Elijah poured her a glass of tea, happy to do anything to serve his beautiful woman. She accepted the offered glass, took a sip, then relaxed back into the chair.

"I've been thinking," she said in a casual tone. "Joining the Black Militia for Union Victory, although noble, was not the right choice for me."

Elijah chuckled to himself. This woman. His woman. Full of surprises. No matter what she wanted to do, he would support her.

"Tell me what the right choice for you is."

"I don't think I told you yet. The reason I wanted to join the militia in the first place was because of a promise Ruth, Abby, and I made during our poker night. We decided we all wanted to help the Union win the war. But I think I need to bend the rules a bit."

She set the glass down on the side table next to her chair and turned to face him head-on. Excitement, determination, and conviction shone brightly in her alluring, dark brown eyes.

"Go on. I am intrigued. Tell me what you would like to do instead."

"I want to help newly freed colored women transition to life in the North. To create a safe place for them. This war will end, and the Union will come out victorious. I have no doubt about that. And when it does, I want to be the anchor in the upheaving storm those women will face."

Elijah sat back in his chair, rubbing a hand over his bearded chin, pretending to think about what she said. He almost laughed out loud when Henrietta scooted closer and closer to the edge of her chair, waiting with bated breath for his thoughts on her new idea.

"That sounds wonderful. Whatever you need me to do, I will help you bring your vision to life."

He didn't think it was possible, but Henrietta's smile grew wider and more brilliant, making her gorgeous face truly stunning. She glanced at the front door, then leaned over the arm of her chair and kissed him. Elijah cupped the sides of her face, deepening the kiss. Before he was ready, she pulled back, keeping her lips just out of reach from his.

"Marry me here and now," she said, her smile becoming sensual and coy.

"We will need a preacher at the very least."

"I'll tell my grandfather to fetch one. I don't want another day to pass without being your wife. Please. Let's get married tonight."

She didn't have to beg him to marry her. Henrietta was everything he'd wanted and more. He would take her any way he could have her.

Elijah pulled her close for another passionate kiss. Releasing her, he looked deeply into her eyes and said, "You are my greatest treasure. The gift I never thought I'd be lucky enough to be blessed with. I will marry you whenever and wherever you wish."

"Good. Then let's go."

Henrietta hoped up out of her chair and held her hand out to Elijah. He laced his fingers between hers and let her pull him back into the house in search of her grandfather.

From this day forth, he would spend the rest of his life making sure that she knew the unconditional depths of love.

Epilogue

Twenty-two years later, 1885

"God... Darn... Tarnation," Henrietta howled, hopping on one foot, the other throbbing in pain.

How many times had she warned her daughter, Orla, about leaving her toys lying about? Especially, the tiny, pointy, wooden farm animals she begged Elijah to carve for her. Henrietta had half a mind to toss them all out with the waste. Only the endless days of listening to Orla's tortured wailing and whimpering over the loss of her beloved playthings kept her from doing it.

Henrietta hobbled to the corner of the nursery and snatched up the basket Orla was supposed to return her toys to when she finished playing. She tossed each of the offending figurines into their rightful home with more force than necessary.

"Don't worry, Mama. I promise to put my toys away," Orla had said, during her imploring speech about why she deserved even more of the frivolous trinkets.

"I'll make sure she does," Elijah had said, coming to their daughter's aid, as he always did.

And there Henrietta had stood. Confronted by two, equally adorable pleading faces. She'd never had a chance. Hence, why she currently cleaned up after her ten-year-old daughter, while said child and her father were nowhere to be found. Henrietta straightened at the sound of a loud, almost pounding knock on the front door.

"I'll get it, Mama," her eldest daughter, Clara, announced from the drawing room.

"Thank you, my love," Henrietta called back.

She made quick work of picking up the rest of the scattered toys, then went to see who'd come to call. Walking down the hall, she slowed her steps, examining the scene unfolding in her doorway. A handsome young man that

Henrietta had never seen before smiled at Clara, chatting with her about something she couldn't hear.

Something about him was vaguely familiar, but she couldn't figure out what.

My goodness! Henrietta gasped, her hand flying to her chest.

If she hadn't heard it with her own ears, she wouldn't have believed it. Her hard as nails daughter had giggled. She'd giggled in the girlish way of a woman sweet on a man.

"Well, who do we have here?" Henrietta asked, closing the distance between herself and the young couple.

They both started as if she'd appeared out of thin air, instead of slowly walking up to them.

"Oh... um... Mother. This is Viscount Clifton. My Lord, this is my mother Mrs. Henrietta Byrne."

"Pleasure to meet you, madam," he said, taking Henrietta's hand and placing a quick kiss on her knuckles.

Henrietta noted his impeccable posture, well-groomed appearance, and the educated upper-class lilt of his British accent.

"The pleasure is mine," she replied, keeping her expression polite. "What brings you to our home on this lovely afternoon?"

"I come on behalf of my father, The Earl of Devon. You knew him as Richard. He said the two of you had the good fortune of meeting in your youth."

Alarm bells trumpeted in Henrietta's head. She took a reflexive step in front of Clara, wedging herself between her and their guest. If this was Richard's son, she wanted him to stay as far away from Clara as possible. Richard had been the most devilish rake she'd ever met. He probably had changed little over the years, and the apple never fell far from the tree.

"Yes, I knew your father. How is he?"

"Very well. Thank you for asking."

She crossed her arms, making a point that the pleasantries were now finished. "And what exactly is the nature of your visit?"

"My father sent me with a message."

"Which is?" He handed her a folded piece of paper. Henrietta read the note aloud. "'I've sent my son to collect on your promise. Please assist him in finding a bride.'"

Henrietta crumpled the note and closed her eyes. "Clara, go retrieve your father and brother. I believe they are looking after Mrs. Walters and her new babe." Her sharp tone left no room for arguments.

"Yes, Mama." Clara scurried off to do as her mother had asked.

Pinching the bridge of her nose, Henrietta released an exasperated sigh. What had she been thinking in her youth? Promise. Promises. None of which ever worked in her favor. She opened her eyes, pursed her lips, and scrutinized the young man standing on her front porch.

"Come in." She stepped aside, giving him space to enter the house. "Let's figure out what to do with you."

Dear Reader,

The inspiration my new series, Ladies of the Civil War, came to me while visiting the Confederate Prison Camp site in Andersonville, Georgia. It was such a fascinating experience being there and seeing where the Union Soldiers were kept and what they experienced. While reading an info card I learned that a few women had been prisoners alongside the men (usually with their husbands).

The gift shop had a book They Fought Like Demons: Women Soldiers in the American Civil War by DeAnne Blanton. I purchased the book and was absolutely fascinated. There were women that fought in battles while pregnant! I mean come on, that's so cool! I wanted to explore these types of stories in my writing. Thus, my new series was born. I wanted to highlight the things women did to help contribute to the war efforts. It has been such a wonderful learning experience and I am so excited to share these stories with you.

If you're a new reader of my work, I've created a universe with the characters and side characters from the novels in all my books. So, this is goodbye to Elijah and Henrietta for now, but not for forever.

Again, thank you so much for reading! I am literally nothing without you.

Until the next story,

G.S. Catt

Other books by Author G.S. Carr

The Cost of Love Series:
The Cost of Hope
The Cost of Atonement
The Cost of Rebellion

Ladies of the Civil War Series:
Lady of Secrets
Lady of Disguise – Coming spring 2020
Lady of Healing - Coming summer 2020
Lady of Faith - Coming winter 2020

About the Author

Important facts:
- Allergic to vegetables, and lover of thinly sliced fried potatoes (also misclassified as French Fries)
- Nerd who would love to build a website, as much as, write a book

From an early age, G.S. Carr consumed books like they were the air she needed to survive. Now she writes love stories that will make you laugh, cry, and shake your fist at the air screaming, "Wwwhhhhyyyy?!?!"

Keep in touch:
www.gscarr.com
www.facebook.com/authorgscarr
info@authorgscarr.com

CPSIA information can be obtained
at www.ICGtesting.com
Printed in the USA
LVHW051501070720
659996LV00002B/212